ELVIRA FERNANDEZ

ISBN 979-8-89186-999-8

This book has been published with all efforts taken to make the material error-free after the consent of the author. However, the author and the publisher do not assume and hereby disclaim any liability to any party for any loss, damage, or disruption caused by errors or omissions, whether such errors or omissions result from negligence, accident, or any other cause.

While every effort has been made to avoid any mistake or omission, this publication is being sold on the condition and understanding that neither the author nor the publishers or printers would be liable in any manner to any person by reason of any mistake or omission in this publication or for any action taken or omitted to be taken or advice rendered or accepted on the basis of this work. For any defect in printing or binding the publishers will be liable only to replace the defective copy by another copy of this work then available.

For

Poornima Kapoor

whose interest has never waned

in the stories I weave.

Acknowledgements

I will give thanks to you, Lord, with all my heart; I will tell of all your wonderful deeds. Psalm 9:1

My heart overflows with gratitude to the Almighty God who stands by my side and holds me every time I fall. Without His will, neither can the moon set nor the sun rise. He shuts doors no one can open and opens doors no one can shut. I love to believe that He approves of what I'm doing and blesses the work of my mind and hands.

No words of appreciation or acknowledgement can ever do justice to the efforts of my teachers, my mentors who have moulded me over my formative years. Their generosity and selfless spirit has brought me to where I stand today. Their love for perfection and insistence on striving harder instilled invaluable habits in me. Their unwavering presence at my book launches and their blessings make me richer. I hope that someday I'll make them proud.

My mother has been a great pillar of strength in all these years and months. She amazes me with her intuition and foresight at times. Well, that's what you call a mother's heart, it senses before it sees. Lots of love to my dear sister, Veronica and her prince charming, my brother-in-law Ronald who have an amazing love story themselves. Probably, some day that will form the basis of one of my novels. My darling nephew, Ethan and his stories of tooth fairies have re-kindled a belief in those magical beings, so, much gratitude to the handsome, little boy. And then, many 'thank-yous' to my entire family and especially to my cousin Conrad who by God's grace could make it to my previous book launch. His feedback and his efforts to share his friends' reviews of my novels can never go unnoticed.

I can't fail to acknowledge the immense support from Ma'am Rajni Saxena who's been that bossy elder sister who'll fight for you and won't hesitate to fight with you when you refuse to see things. Coming in close, is a friend who's not read a single story, poem or book I've written but his blind trust in my work is unbelievable. I'm referring to none other than Prakash Manghnani Sir. He's always there whenever I call for help. Ma'am Kavita Mathur has been an inspiration and still continues to be with her grace and eerie precision and foresight. I'll never be able to say 'thank you' enough for her guidance and motherly love. I'm also grateful to Ma'am Sandhya Bhaduaria, Ma'am Bini Sunu and Ma'am Meenakshi Malhotra who stand strongly by my side at every book launch.

A special mention for Retd. Lt. Gen. Surendra Kulkarni Sir who by his presence at my last book launch made the experience an unforgettable one. Sir mentioned a vintage car rally when I met him a couple of days later and I've tried to immortalize the conversation by introducing a similar event in the novel. This fatherly figure, a man of his word, and brimming with ideas, is a huge inspiration.

Amongst my readers and young friends I can't forget to mention Deepti Chinaria, Dr. Achal Deep Dubey, Sakshi Mehra, Akrishi Bhiryani, Anushree Agarwal, Megha Kanani, Khushi Ramrakhyani, Nirat Khandelwal, Nitya Rochani, and Tejal Choudhary. I may be guilty of having forgotten to name some dear ones but I assure them that they still live in my heart. Thank you for all your love and kind reviews, dear readers. Your thoughtful choice of words helps me to persevere on these lonely journeys of crafting stories and etching characters. I'll keep looking forward to your valuable feedbacks, they truly mean a lot.

Saving the best for the last I'm immensely grateful to Poornima Kapoor who's been there! I sometimes wonder if I bore her to death with endless plots, stories and projects. This young lady knows how to keep her calm, churns out amazing advice (at her age) and goes that extra mile for me. Well, do I need to tell everyone that the exquisite cover is yet another creation by this wonderful artist? Enjoy the magical beauty of the book cover before you journey into the pages.

Introduction

"We are all broken... that's how the light gets in." Ernest Hemmingway

It's autumn and the days are getting colder. I'm down with a terrible cold and cough. And hence, I don't feel like doing much except reading, watching some good movies, listening to English and Hindi songs from the 50's, 60's and 70's and of course writing when I'm not sleeping. A bowl of hot soup with noodles or a mug of steaming coffee is just the thing to keep me happy these days. The weak sunshine isn't much of a blessing to me at the moment. My garden however, has a mind of its own and is luxuriating in the early chill of the season. The bougainvilleas have put out light mauve, dark pink and dark maroon blossoms and are basking in the sun's tepid warmth. Petunias are beginning to show up in white, red, pink and deep purple. And, the roses are just making their majestic presence felt with that heady fragrance. The chrysanthemums are budding and I hope to see their white and yellow beauty revealed in another week.

After a short walk in my garden here I am gazing at my laptop and listening to my heart, telling you about

Ella and her prince charming. It's really dreadful to have your heart all cracked, especially by someone you'd come to trust so much. Who says it's going to be easy to start believing in someone else again? You don't want to feel like you've been made a fool again, you don't want to wait again, you don't want to fight again, you don't want to let heart wrenching sobs shake your body again, you don't want to sit awake at night wondering where you went wrong. Well, Ella's no different. She's had enough and she's happy to live a life being 'the good' to others instead of waiting for 'something good' to happen to her. Her fairy godmother, Lucia Merryweather however has different plans for her dear goddaughter. She's adamant that Ella should have her very own 'happy ever after'. It's soon going to be Christmas time in the city and we all wish and hope for some Christmas magic. Will Lucia's conviction and a little magical help open Ella's heart to the man she truly deserves? In the simple, lucid style that I prefer over others, I welcome you to be a part of yet another romantic story.

While you eagerly turn the pages to know more about Ella, her fairy godmother and her prince charming, I'm off to engage in a dialogue with Meowsie, another stray cat who's decided he wants to claim ownership of me and my garden. This white cat with selective black markings is just as loud as his predecessors who wouldn't tolerate being ignored. He's already complaining, asking for his mid-day meal. Dear Readers, please excuse me, I've got to leave you here! Do I need to remind you that I'll be looking forward to your reviews via messages, calls, posts on different social media channels or on online shopping sites? I wouldn't mind if you meet me in person and share your experiences of reading this latest novel – a fairytale romance, and a Christmas love story. Those of you who would like to mail me, please do so, my email address is: elvifernandez08@gmail.com

I'll see you again sometime soon when I bring you my next novel, till then take good care of yourselves!

Happy Reading!

Elvira Fernandez

"And... that's L-O-V-E."

"Good going, Gabriella. Now I can make my word. I love this game of scrabble. It helps me to practice my spellings. And, here is my word."

"What's this word?" Gabriella asked looking at the board in amazement. "What's D-O-T-T-E-R?"

"Ahh... My dear Gabriella, it's an old German word for daughter. It's quite acceptable for a game of scrabble."

"Really! Lucia, you bring the weirdest words and spellings to the game. By the way, this reminds me, how's your goddaughter? Any news?" queried Gabriella.

"Ella...? O dear! She's still not willing to believe in love and because of that here am I... stuck, playing scrabble and earth gazing," sighed Lucia looking down through the clouds.

"Hmm... I quite understand the feeling. It's not easy being a fairy godmother, isn't it? You cannot make a move till she believes in that feeling," Gabriella said. "And, here's my next word, C-H-A-R-M-I-N-G."

"How I wish my dear Ella finds her Prince Charming and falls in love with him. I'll be there to give them those butterflies in the stomach and that little magical push but..."

"But?"

"... but for that Ella has to first believe in love, Gabriella. The girl just runs from the feeling," Lucia said quietly.

"You know you can't blame her, Lucia, after all that she's been through..."

"Yes, yes. I know Gabriella. The girl has seen so much... her parents... friends around... her own heart has been broken," Lucia said placing another word on the board. "L-U-C-K-Y."

"I'm sure your Ella will be lucky in love, soon. She deserves to be loved and cherished, she has the kindest of hearts," Gabriella said softly, looking at her friend.

"Yes, she is kind and gentle. Surely somewhere there is someone who will open her eyes and heart to love once again," Lucia smiled.

"Amen to that, Lucia. Amen!" Gabriella said fervently.

"My dear godchild Ella, may your heart be touched by love soon. And, when it does... the snow will melt, flowers will blossom and fill the air with a sweet fragrance. Birds and bees will sing songs of love and togetherness, and rabbits with hares will dance and make merry," Lucia whispered softly. "I wish with my whole heart that you find your true love, your soul mate."

"Is that a prophecy, Lucia?" Gabriella looked at her friend in admiration.

"Did it sound like one?" Lucia asked in amazement. "I thought I was making a wish with my breath and being."

"Part of it did sound like it."

"Whatever it may be, I only hope Ella believes in love, only then can I help her receive it," Lucia said making another word. "H-O-P-E."

"Lucia... it's my turn. Why did you make a word? When will you stop playing out of turn?" Gabriella grumbled.

"Oh, I'm sorry dear. But it's a good word, isn't it? Hope! It makes life worthwhile. Doesn't it?" Lucia smiled. "What did that Emily Dickinson say? 'Hope is a bird singing in a tree'. She was a famous poet."

"Lucia, for God's sake... Emily Dickinson said, 'Hope' is the thing with feathers. I remember her poem quite well," Gabriella groaned as she placed words on the Scrabble Board. "F-O-R-E-V-E-R."

"Lovely! I love this word... 'FOREVER'. It's wonderful to say... And, they lived happily 'forever and ever'. It's one of my favourite phrases," Lucia smiled.

"Yes, like in a fairytale," agreed Gabriella.

"Oh yes, oh yes! My Ella will surely have her very own fairytale... I can feel it. It will be soon... soon. I can't wait for her 'Once upon a time' to begin," Lucia looked down once again through the clouds and smiled. "I can just feel it."

"Hannah, please take the order from table two."

"I'll be there in a minute, Ella."

"Hello, Mrs. Stephens. How are you? How are the kids?" Ella smiled at one of her regular customers.

"I'm fine. The kids are great too. How are you?"

"I'm doing great. How can I help you?" Ella enquired cheerfully wiping her hands to a small towel.

"I was looking for a cake for my younger one. But..." Mrs. Stephens hesitated.

Ella looked at her and smiled. She knew the family wasn't doing too well. "I've just the thing for little Liam. Just wait a moment."

Ella walked to the display and came back with a two pound chocolate mousse cake.

"Ella, this will be too expensive..." Mrs. Stephens looked at the girl before her with a pleasant face, dark brown hair and dark brown eyes, in horror.

"No Mrs. Stephens. It just costs..." Ella mentioned a decent figure and saw the relief wash over the tired face.

"Are you sure, Ella dear?"

"Yes, Mrs. Stephens. It's my cafe, isn't it? How can I not be sure?" Ella laughed. "Shall I write 'Happy Birthday Liam' on it?"

"Yes, that would be great. It's Liam's favourite cake. He loves it," Mrs. Stephens smiled. "God bless you!"

"Do wish Liam on my behalf. Will you? Tell him I'll have his favourite almond cookies at hand when he comes to visit me next," Ella said, quickly packing the cake and slipping in a few chocolates quietly.

"Thank you... Thank you so much!" gushed Mrs. Stephens as she left with her parcel.

"Ella, that cake..." began Hannah only to be shushed kindly.

"It's alright. Little Liam will be happy," Ella smiled at the help who worked with her at her cafe 'Cakes, Coffee and Cookies'.

"If you say so..." Hannah shook her head as she saw a customer entering the cafe. Hannah walked into the room at the back of the cafe which housed a perfectly fitted out kitchen complete with stoves and ovens. The three member staff also had their personal cupboards and sitting space here.

Ella Wilson was the kindest of persons she had ever known. She was much loved by the people of the town, especially the senior citizens and children. She had a kind word for everyone and time to listen to every concern and worry. It was really sad that this beautiful soul had no one to call her own in the world. She lived alone in an ancestral home not far from the cafe. Her parents had passed away within a few months of each other. Hannah recollected those happy days when she, in her late teens had taken up work with the Wilson family. Ella had been a toddler then. Years had passed but she had stayed on, her own family growing, her hair getting grey.

"Hannah, you must take a break now," called Ella cheerfully. "You've been on your toes since morning."

"I will as soon as I get this last batch of freshly baked croissants into the display," Hannah said carrying out a loaded tray.

A delicious aroma wafted in with her and the golden brown crescents called for attention.

The bell at the entrance tinkled cheerfully as the local sheriff in his uniform walked in – a portly figure, fatherly and the proud owner of a broad smile.

"Hello Ella! All good?"

"All good, Sheriff. Shall I get the usual?"

"Yes, a cup of black coffee. And, what's that lovely smell?"

"Croissants!" said Hannah. "Want one, Jack?"

"Hello Hannah! I could surely do with one. My wife didn't pack me any lunch today. Jack Junior is down with a terrible cold, cough and fever. The missus was up all night had to take him to the doctor," Jack said sitting down at a table near the window and taking off his gloves. "It's a cold day. Thank God there's no snow."

"Here's your coffee," smiled Ella. "I'll get you an egg salad with your croissant. Tell Michelle I'll be with her in the evening today. She'll need help with little Wendy, won't she?"

Sheriff Jack looked at her in admiration, "You will? That's so kind of you. I'm on special duty till night. A meeting of the big shots, with our Mayor! Some huge event will be coming up this spring. You're a brick, Ella. Isn't she Hannah?"

"Yes, she is. That's why everyone loves her so much," Hannah said warmly.

"Stop it! Next you all will be crowning me Saint Ella," laughed Ella as she walked to the kitchen.

~

"Hi Ella, it's jolly kind of you to offer to help me with the kids today evening. Jack told me you would come after five. The cafe?" Michelle queried opening the front door and letting in the cold air with Ella.

"No problem. Hannah and Jim are there to look after the customers. How's Jack Junior?" Ella asked taking off the overcoat and gloves. Her cheeks were pink from the cold and Michelle stared at her for a few moments thinking how pretty she looked, before replying.

"Oh... Jackie is feeling much better. His temperature is down. Doctor Saunders thinks it a mild cold and cough. He'll be right as rain in a day or two. Come let's have a cup of tea in the kitchen before both the kids wake up. I'll serve them their supper then," Michelle led the way to the cosy kitchen.

"I could do with a cup of tea. It's been a tiring day. Lots of tourists visit our town during the winter months," Ella said sitting on a chair at the table.

"Hmm... that's true. This year we'll be having many still coming in during spring too. Jack was saying something big is coming up," Michelle placed a tray with slices of fruit cake and the tea cups on the table before sitting down herself.

"Yes. Sheriff did mention something today afternoon," Ella nodded and took a heartening sip from her cup. "But we do have a fair crowd in spring every year, don't we?"

"Yes, we do. But this year it will be more than that. It will be a good opportunity for our town, I heard. More chances of increasing the income," Michelle said biting into a slice.

"Definitely! Our Mayor is a clever man and so thoughtful. I truly admire him," Ella said.

"Jack says that too..." Michelle paused and got up from the table. "Looks like Wendy is up."

"Good morning Ella! Thanks for the help all these days, young lady. You've been God sent. Michelle and I can't thank you enough," Jack thanked Ella profusely as he walked into the cafe.

"Sheriff, please don't mention it. I did nothing at all," Ella paused from what she was doing and smiled warmly.

"If 'nothing' means being puked on and not making a face, helping to feed two cranky toddlers, giving a helping hand with suppers, laundry and... what not, then thank you for 'nothing'."

"Oh hush now! You're embarrassing me," Ella blushed and began wiping the glass counter vigorously.

"Ok. I won't embarrass you but I've got something for you. Here, have a look!" Jack placed a flyer on the counter.

"What's this?" asked Hannah who was getting Jack's black coffee.

"Hmm... sounds interesting," Ella who had been reading said. "There's supposed to be a Spring Festival in our town this year. The Whitman Castle will be open to visiting tourists after five years. In its grounds there will be a vintage car rally on the opening day, after that the cars will be kept on display for a fortnight."

"These cars are expected to be extremely ancient. They'll be driven in from far and near. There will be an award for the best maintained one," Jack said sipping the hot brew.

"But Lord Whitman… he passed away, if I'm not mistaken," Ella said softly, still looking at the flyer.

"Hmm…" Jack swallowed another sip before answering. "Yes, he did. The Mayor managed to get in touch with his successor, a nephew, the new Lord Whitman who lives somewhere in foreign lands. The guy has agreed to have the castle and grounds opened up to the public again."

"How wonderful! That place always had something magical about it. It seems to pull in crowds and especially lovers," Hannah clasped her hands happily.

"I've no idea about lovers but for us it definitely means business," laughed Ella. "I'll apply to the Town Council for a stall in the grounds. There will be different stalls being set up, Sheriff? I remember father telling mother about booking a stall every year for the festival. Mother and I used to spend such a happy time on the grounds. There used to be so much going on for almost a month."

"Oh yes, of course. That's why I wanted to show you this flyer. You're a very practical and level-headed person," Jack nodded in appreciation.

"Will the new Lord Whitman come to the inauguration of the Festival?" queried Hannah.

"No idea, Hannah. Maybe, maybe not. It seems he lives on the other side of the world. Has his business set up in different parts of the globe, leads a busy life. I heard it took a lot of effort on the part of the Mayor to get in touch with him," Jack answered.

"But before they open the castle and the grounds, a lot of renovation work will be required. Won't it?" Ella asked thoughtfully. "It's been closed for five years."

"Yes sure, it will. The council is working out all those details. It will take two or three months; hence the festival will be scheduled for early April. These flyers will be pasted around the town by today evening. The tourists who are here will be able to make plans or pass on the word to their friends," Jack said keeping his mug on the counter.

"I wonder if the new Lord Whitman is young or old," Hannah said aloud.

"Well! I have no idea. And, how does that matter as long as he's helping the town to grow like the former Lord Whitman," Jack shrugged as he prepared to leave.

"For all we know, Hannah, he may be middle-aged with a pot belly and a nose stuck up in the air," laughed Ella. "Too busy counting his money to come to a small town and meet people around here."

"Quite an imagination!" laughed Jack, walking to the door. "Goodbye, ladies!"

"Maybe..." sighed Hannah.

"Aww... Don't sound so upset," Ella said hugging her.

"How nice it would be, if he's young, dashing, handsome and single! He could sweep you off your feet..." Hannah said dreamily.

"Hannah! How many romantic movies are you watching these days? I know your boys are in university and only both, you and Jim are at home. You're getting overly imaginative," laughed Ella.

"Ella dear, you deserve the best. There's no one in our town worth you. The tourists that come in... I had thought there would be some chance of a good man coming some day but that's not happening either..." Hannah said looking at Ella tenderly.

"Hannah, I'm so blessed that you concern yourself with me so much but... please don't worry about me. I'm fine. I'm happy living the life I am. See, I have you all taking care of me," Ella smiled.

"I will never forgive that horrible man you were to marry. He was never meant for you. He was always interested in your cafe and the money you earned. The moment that rich cousin of yours came to attend your wedding, he took to her and eloped! Horrible, horrible creature!" Hannah's eyes sparkled with anger.

"Hannah... Hannah... calm down. Here, drink some water. Forget them. Aren't we happy here together? What would have I done if this had to happen after the wedding?" Ella reasoned with her.

"That's all alright. But after this incident you've shut your heart to love and the possibility to a happy married life, Ella. You think I don't understand. I wish your dear parents were alive. Your mother was such a caring person. She took me under her wing years ago, she would reason with me and explain things so well," Hannah said quietly.

"I miss them too, Hannah. But I have you, and that's good, isn't it? You're here to take care of me and reason with me," Ella spoke gently.

"Yes, but it's not the same, Ella dear. You know it isn't!" Hannah insisted.

"Hannah..." began Ella soothingly when the bell at the door tinkled joyfully and a family of tourists stepped in talking nineteen to the dozen.

"Hannah, is everything alright?"

"All good, Ella. Jim is looking after the Cafe. I just had a talk with him. It was quite noisy, many customers in there too," Hannah smiled arranging the cupcakes.

"Wow! This Spring Festival has actually turned out to be quite interesting. Look, the grounds are so crowded," Ella said waving a hand.

"Hello... Do you have macaroons? My little boy loves those," a sweet looking lady with a five-year old asked.

"Yes, we do," smiled Ella as Hannah quoted the price.

"Are you enjoying yourself?" queried Ella.

"Very much! We've been inside the castle. It's breathtakingly beautiful. The grounds are so well kept and the flowers are just blooming everywhere. I'm so happy we came. I loved your town too, so archaic but well maintained with all the modern amenities," the lady gushed. "I absolutely adored the cobbled streets and some of the gabled roof homes. And, there are pretty flowers in profusion everywhere."

"I'm so glad you're happy being here. Would you also like some lemonade?" asked Ella.

"Yes, two glasses please. How much?"

Hannah told her with a smile and handed over the change.

"I've clicked a few pictures; I'm a photographer you see. Could I have one of you both in your stall?" the lady asked politely.

"Yes, why not!" Ella agreed. The woman took a few quick shots of them and their wares.

"Thank you so much. This Spring Festival and the vintage car rally has attracted many photographers from far and near. I'm glad I got some really good clicks," the woman supplied checking her shots and showing Ella. "You look beautiful."

"Thank you so much. By the way, I'm Ella and this is Hannah. Do visit 'Cakes, Coffee and Cookies', my cafe if you're around," Ella said with a smile.

"I'm Julie and this is my son, Jamie. Sure, I will. See you later. Bye!" the woman waved as she walked on.

"Seriously! This vintage car rally has drawn in the crowds," Hannah observed looking in the direction where around twenty cars stood. People thronged the area either clicking pictures, gazing with rapt attention or reading the placards.

"Hmm... Newspaper and news channel reporters were here too on the day of the inauguration. Only the new Lord Whitman was missing, it seems. There was much speculation about that too," Ella said adjusting a cupcake with its pink frosting on the tray.

"Yes, someone was saying he's an invalid, confined to his wheelchair for years. He has long white hair and knobbly fingers and wrists," Hannah provided sitting down on a chair.

"And, I remember you saying only a few months ago that 'he' could be young, handsome and dashing," laughed Ella.

"I said, I 'wished' he would be young, handsome and dashing," pouted Hannah. "I only wanted what's best for you."

"I know... I know... I'm just teasing you," Ella settled down in the chair next to hers. "Anyway, we better have our sandwiches and lemonade before the crowds start coming it. There's a slight lull because of the lunch time. Where's the picnic basket we brought with us, Hannah?"

"It's under the table. I packed us some tomato and cucumber sandwiches today. I'm glad we got this spot under this huge oak tree. It's so shady and cool here. It truly feels like having a picnic. There are few slices of fruit cake also," Hannah said slipping off her shoes and luxuriating in the feel of having the soft grass beneath her bare feet. "Hmm... this is heavenly."

"You're right. The colourful tents are great but I like being under this tree. Mmmm... These sandwiches taste delicious," Ella munched her sandwich with relish. "Isn't that old Mrs. Hendricks?"

"Yes. Looks like her scarves and stoles are much in demand. Quite a crowd around her even during lunch time," nodded Hannah.

"But why is she alone? Where's her son?" queried Ella looking at her, still munching.

"He may have gone home to his wife. She just had a baby last week," Hannah said.

"Ah yes! I think I'll go and help her for a bit, till her son gets back. I'll take her a sandwich also and a lemonade," Ella said standing up and dusting the crumbs from her white cotton dress with printed yellow daisies.

"Yes dear. She looks like she can do with a little help," Hannah agreed.

"You'll be alright on your own?" asked Ella wrapping a sandwich in paper napkins and filling a paper cup with lemonade.

"Of course, Ella. I'll manage just fine. There won't be many customers till tea-time. Her son should be back by then, I think."

~

"Hello Mrs. Hendricks. I got you a sandwich and some lemonade. Have a quick snack while I attend to your customers," Ella put an arm around the old shoulders and felt the relief.

"Ahh... Ella! Thank you dear. I was feeling so thirsty," the old lady took the paper cup and sipped eagerly.

She watched with her beady eyes while Ella smiled and chatted with the tourists, told them the prices, cleverly fobbed off attempts at bargaining, packed the sold goods in brown paper bags, collected the money, and handed over the change.

"Feeling refreshed?" asked Ella when she caught her looking at her. "Please rest for a couple of minutes more. I hope I'm doing all the right things."

"You're doing a wonderful job!" announced Mrs. Hendricks with a smile and wondered for the thousandth time why this beautiful and kind hearted girl wasn't hitched as yet.

Finally the last of the customers left with their parcels and Ella collapsed in a chair beside the old woman. "Whew! That was quite a crowd. I'm glad your stall is doing well even during lunchtime."

"I'm grateful to God, He's been very kind. This has been a marvellous opportunity to showcase my woollen scarves and stoles. All of them are handmade from the best quality wool," Mrs. Hendricks said.

"I completely agree," nodded Ella.

"Our Mayor has been very thoughtful. I must remember to thank him when I get a chance to meet him," Mrs. Hendricks smoothed a crease from her brown skirt.

"Many want to thank the new Lord Whitman for his generosity but he couldn't make it. I heard he's quite old and an invalid, he can't move around much. Lives at the other side of the world," Ella said.

"Is it so?" queried a male voice with interest.

Both the women had been lost in conversation and failed to notice this man who was studying the various scarves and stoles. They looked at him then, in surprise.

"Sorry?" queried Ella.

"No... You were talking about the new Lord Whitman. I was wondering if that's so," shrugged the man with a head of dark hair. He had twinkling eyes, chocolate brown like her chocolate cakes. A well built physique said he spent hours in a gym. He seemed to be laughing at her.

"It's not good to eavesdrop," said Ella sternly, turning pink when she realized she had been staring rudely.

The man raised his dark eyebrows in surprise, "I thought it wasn't good to spread rumours either."

"Excuse me. How do you know that's not the truth?" challenged Ella.

"Well, since you've neither met the man nor seen him, it's not good to gossip about him. After all, he's taken a huge decision to open the castle and its grounds for the festival," the man said.

"Do you know Lord Whitman?" asked Ella. "Have you met him?"

"Well..." the man hesitated.

"Good! I thought so," nodded Ella. "Now that you've accepted, indirectly, that you've neither met him nor seen him, please stop poking your nose into conversations that don't involve you."

Mrs. Hendricks drew in a sharp breath. She had never seen or heard their dear Ella speak like this before.

The man however seemed to be amused. He stared in open admiration at her pink cheeks.

"Did anyone ever tell you, your eyes begin to emit sparks when you're angry?" he said softly.

"Excuse me..." spluttered Ella in rage.

"You're excused," he said and waved cheerfully as he walked on.

"What the hell!" Ella muttered as she shrugged in exasperation.

"Calm down, my dear. Sit... Drink some water. Are you alright?" Mrs. Hendricks looked in concern and interest at this girl whom they had always seen so quiet and composed. This was a new side she had seen today and she was thrilled. Their Miss Ella did have a furious temper. And, it was this handsome stranger who had ignited the sparks. Who was he?

~

"Who was he?" queried Hannah with interest.

"I've no idea who he was... is..." grumbled Ella. "All I know is that he's mighty rude. I hope I never set eyes on him ever again otherwise I'll have something to say to him."

"Are you talking about me?" asked a voice she remembered hearing half an hour ago.

Ella spun around with her mouth open and stared at the same young man with twinkling chocolate brown eyes.

"You... You... Are you following me?" she looked at him suspiciously through narrowed eyes.

"Yes... Me... Me..." he said nonchalantly. "Why would I follow you? I was told this stall sold the most delicious cream cakes. So, I've come here for a slice. By the way, what are you doing here? Spreading more rumours or just *following me*?"

"What? The first thing is, I DON'T gossip. Secondly, why would *I* follow you? And technically, that's not even possible," Ella said hotly.

"And, why's that?" he queried sweetly.

"...because I was here before you," Ella said with a huff.

"Well, that seems to make sense. Now, if you'd excuse me I'd like to speak to this lovely lady here and get a slice of the heavenly cream cakes she sells," he dismissed Ella and turned to Hannah who was looking from one to the other with interest.

Ella looked at him in astonishment, her mouth open.

"I suggest you shut your mouth before flies find their way in," he said bending over the delicious spread.

"You... you..." Ella fumed and fumbled for words.

"Oh... Well... Hello..." Hannah chimed in. "How can I help you, sir?"

"Hello... I would like a slice of your 'most' yummiest cream cake," smiled the stranger as he spoke to Hannah.

"Right away, sir. Would you like to eat it now or shall I pack it?" Hannah asked as was customary.

"I'd like to eat it now, Miss...?" the stranger dimpled charmingly. "How can one resist the temptation of cream cakes?"

"Hannah, call me Hannah," smiled the loyal assistant, obviously quite taken up. "Here's the slice, sir."

"I've always loved that name. Please don't call me 'sir'. It makes me feel ancient, probably like the owner of this castle. My name is Andrew Anderson," he said taking the paper plate she offered him.

Ella snorted.

"Who is she?" Andrew leaned closer to Hannah and queried in a loud whisper. "She's so rude and a big gossip monger. You mustn't allow her around your stall. It would be bad for business."

Hannah choked back laughter as she looked at Ella's outraged face.

She cleared her throat and spoke up, "Let me introduce you. This is Ella Wilson, the owner of the cafe 'Cakes, Coffee and Cookies'. It's quite popular in our town."

"Ah... I see. So, technically speaking you're the owner of this stall, Miss Wilson. Interesting!" Andrew said looking at her thoughtfully.

"What's interesting about that?" Ella queried curiously.

"Nothing much except... it suddenly occurred to me that cafes are the best spots for gossips. No wonder..." he broke off to spoon some cake into his mouth. "Hmm... delightful! This is the best I've ever tasted."

"You're terrible!" Ella exclaimed angrily.

"Terrible? Why? Just because I praised this confectionery from your cafe?" Andrew shook his head disapprovingly. "How rude! Where are your manners? You should have smiled and thanked me. Isn't it, Hannah?"

"Don't you go seeking Hannah's approval and draw her into *your* rude conversation. You know quite well, I wasn't speaking about the cake," Ella glowered at him.

"Then? What were you talking about?" he asked sweetly, eating another spoonful.

"About... about... you calling me a gossip monger," Ella said angrily.

"Did I? I just said, 'cafes are the best spots for gossips'. Is there anything wrong about that?" Andrew turned to Hannah with an innocent look on his face.

"You...you..." Ella began.

"Yes... Me... Me..." Andrew said looking at her seriously. "You seem to have a very limited vocabulary in spite of owning a cafe."

Ella shut her eyes, took a deep breath and said, "I suggest you leave if you want to be rude."

"Why should I leave? I want another piece of this delectable cake. And, if I'm not wrong the saying goes, 'The customer is always right'. So, if I'm disturbing you, *you* leave. I'm pretty sure Hannah has no problem in attending to my requirements," Andrew said sweetly, leaning against the table on which the food stuff was displayed.

"Very well. I'm going. I can't stand you for a minute longer. Hannah, I'll be back when he leaves," Ella tossed her head and walked away, her dark brown hair pulled in a high ponytail swinging angrily.

"She's the sweetest person around. I've no idea why..." Hannah broke off looking at Ella's stiff back as she walked towards the vintage cars.

"No doubt, she is," agreed Andrew solemnly and then laughed. "I seem to have touched a wrong chord. But it's fun to tease someone. I miss my younger sister. It's been a while that I've had such a happy banter."

"You were pulling her legs? Well, I did feel you were but I wasn't sure," smiled Hannah.

"Yes, I was. Someone who bakes such delightful cakes cannot be a gossip or a dumb wit. I'm sure of that," Andrew smiled warmly at Hannah.

"You're right. Here's another slice for you. Ella is loved by everyone in our town. She's kind, generous and a real sweetheart. I wish she could find someone as loving as her. The pity is God seems to have stopped creating those types of young men," Hannah looked him eagerly.

"Aren't there any of those kinds around here?" Andrew asked tucking in.

"No... No. What do you do for a living?" queried Hannah.

"Ahh... I'm a photographer. I heard about this Spring Festival and the vintage car rally, so I thought I could get some wonderful pictures for my exhibition in autumn this year," Andrew said eating with gusto.

"Do photographers make good money?" asked Hannah.

Andrew smiled, "Yes, in a way. Enough to live comfortably."

"You don't seem to be married," observed Hannah looking at the ring finger of his left hand.

"Yes, because I'm not married," laughed Andrew.

"You're just the kind of person who would be perfect for our Ella. I had pictured someone like you – tall, dark, handsome, with a sense of humour, someone who would rattle her yet love her..." Hannah drifted off looking into the distance, at Ella speaking to the tourists near the cars.

"O dear! She's a spitfire! I would be terrified of her," laughed Andrew good naturedly looking at Ella too. "Anyway, I must get a move on. I want a few good shots before the sun sets. See you again. I'll be around for another week or so."

"Goodbye, Andrew! Sure, see you again," waved Hannah cheerfully.

She smiled when she saw him look in the direction where Ella was still speaking to the same tourists, as he walked away.

"Hi there!"

"You again?"

"Yes, me again," said Andrew.

"What do you want?" queried Ella bad naturedly.

"Nothing much, except some bread and butter with hot tea. I think that would do perfectly well for a light breakfast to begin a wonderful morning," Andrew said with a smile.

"I don't think I want to serve you breakfast," Ella folded her arms across her chest and looked at him with a frown.

"Tsk... tsk... bad manners, bad attitude for a businesswoman. I wouldn't do this if I were you," said Andrew in a sing song.

Ella opened her mouth to reply but was interrupted.

"Andrew! How lovely to see you at our cafe," Hannah said happily. "Please make yourself comfortable at one of the tables. I'll be with you in a jiffy to take your order."

"Hannah..." began Ella exasperatedly.

"I know... I know... Ella dear. We're getting late. Anyone can take his order. But I want to. He's such an interesting young man," Hannah said picking up the notepad.

"Thank you, Hannah. I was about to be chased away without breakfast. You're a real life saver," Andrew grinned.

"What? Who was chasing you away?" Hannah looked shocked.

Andrew shoved his hands into his pockets, pursed his lips and nodded in the direction of Ella.

"Ella?" Hannah turned to look at her in surprise. "Why... I never...! You never let anyone go hungry from our cafe. How can you let this fine gentleman leave without eating anything?"

"Fine gentleman? Where? Who are you talking about?" Ella looked surprised.

"Ok... Ok... I suggest you both call a truce and shake hands," Hannah put her hands on her hips and looked at them both. "Come on... come on..."

"I'm ready!" said Andrew at once.

"You wish!" Ella said frowning.

"Come on, Miss Wilson. I accept I was a bit rude yesterday. I'm sorry," Andrew gave her a winsome smile.

"Ella, come on. We all know you're considerate about our guests and especially tourists. You're trying to be someone you're not. And, it doesn't suit you. Where's your sunshine smile? It seems to be hidden behind dark clouds," Hannah cajoled her.

"Alright... alright... You're forgiven Mr. Anderson. Please sit down. We'll get your breakfast ready. Would you like to have a scrambled egg too?" Ella said giving in.

"That's my girl!" clapped Hannah.

"Hannah..." whispered Ella.

"Thank you... I would be grateful," Andrew nodded.

"I'll also get you our special strawberry jam. Ella makes delicious jams," Hannah said excitedly as she hurried towards the kitchen.

~

"I'm so happy the weather is so lovely for the tourists... warm and sunny. It's not very hot either," Hannah said pinning a poster to the tent allotted to them.

"I hope we aren't late," Ella said looking around at the tourists milling around the grounds.

"Not at all dear! It's not yet 9:00 a.m. We managed to get the minivan loaded and reach here in 20 minutes," Hannah said arranging cupcakes with pink and yellow frosting.

"Jim and Joe are real darlings. They're so quick and efficient. Aren't they?" Ella said placing the puff pastries on a plate.

"Yes, they are, dear. But you'll have to agree that Andrew was quite helpful today. He helped to load the minivan," Hannah said wiping her hands to a hand towel.

"We wouldn't have been in a rush hadn't it been for him coming and arguing," Ella said with a frown.

"You're still annoyed with him?"

"No... Only I don't know why I can't seem to..." Ella shrugged. "Well; like him. He somehow seems to irritate me."

"Anger is a prelude to love," mumbled Hannah turning away.

"What?" Ella asked. "What did you say?"

"Nothing... nothing... Just that I hope the weather stays bright and clear," Hannah said innocently.

"Really?" Ella looked at her suspiciously.

"Yes, yes," nodded Hannah.

"Are you open?" asked a twelve year old boy. "Could I have a doughnut?"

"Yes, of course," smiled Ella. "Here you go."

"How much?" he asked.

Hannah told him the amount and gave him a few lemon drops when he handed over the money.

"Lemon drops! Thank you! I love these and so does my sister. You're awesome," he chirped and waved a goodbye.

"Today's Saturday. It looks like we'll have a good crowd pouring in, even from other towns nearby. I heard from the sheriff that the local guest houses are all booked. Even relatives from far and near are visiting families in our town. Everyone's keen on having a look at these vintage cars," Hannah said happily settling down in a chair.

"Good morning, Hannah! Good morning, Ella!"

"Good morning, Pastor James," chorused the two ladies.

"How are you? How's your stall doing?"

"We're good. The stall's doing pretty good. It's the weekend so we're expecting a big crowd," said Ella. "How are you?"

"I'm great. I came along to check the arrangements of the races and games the Church Council is putting up over the weekend. The collections will go to the orphanage," Pastor James said good-naturedly.

"How lovely! What games have they arranged?" asked Hannah.

"Well, there will be musical chairs, housie, hoopla, scrabble, three-legged race, lemon and spoon race and yes, the raffle!" Pastor James spoke with excitement.

"Those are quite a few. When will they begin? I hope I'll get some time to go and witness a race or two," Hannah said expectantly.

"Yes, Pastor James. This sounds really exciting. I'd like to buy a few raffle tickets. Where and who should I get them from?" queried Ella.

"Ahh... The Church Council has set up these tents on the side, near the lake. Mrs. and Mr. Smith are in-charge. The others of course are helping. The younger boys and girls are decorating the place with buntings," Pastor James said happily. "Do come over that side."

"O yes! Definitely!" said Ella.

"Ella dear, you must take part in the game of scrabble. There will be no more than two players on each board.

You're so good at it. In fact, the best from our town," the Pastor said.

"Yes Ella. You must go for it, dear. You should," insisted Hannah.

"I'll try, Pastor James. I can't be away for long from our stall. There'll be a rush today and tomorrow, as you already know..." Ella smiled.

"I know... I know... But there's always a chance. Do try, dear. Now, I must be off. I need to check on the prizes sponsored by the members of our church," Pastor James said turning to walk away.

"Wait a minute, Pastor. How about this walnut and chocolate cake as one of the prizes for a game of scrabble?" Ella asked smiling.

"That would be a delicious prize indeed, my dear. Thank you for your generosity," Pastor James beamed at her.

"I'll come with you now and hand it over to Mrs. and Mr. Smith," Ella said and hurried away to pack the cake in a box. "You'll be fine alone, for a couple of minutes, Hannah?"

"O yes, I will dear. Do register yourself for a game of scrabble and also get me two raffle tickets while you're there," Hannah said eagerly.

"Yes, I'll do that. Alright Pastor James, let's go. I'm ready," Ella held the box with the cake carefully and followed the reverend, her waist long hair drawn into a pony tail, swinging from side to side and shining in the bright spring sunshine.

Hannah watched her lovingly, turned her eyes towards heaven and prayed fervently, "Dear God in heaven, may this kind-hearted girl find her true love. Touch her heart so that it may be opened to welcome love once again."

"Welcome back Ella. How's the day been?" queried Mrs. Smith, a pleasant middle-aged woman.

"Extremely busy, Mrs. Smith. We've already called for chicken sandwiches and lamb burgers twice from the cafe. I wouldn't be able to manage without Hannah, Jim, and Joe. How's everything going on here?" Ella asked looking around.

"We've just finished with the three-legged, and lemon and spoon races. The participants are coming in for the game of scrabble. We'll begin by 3:30. There's fifteen minutes to that," Mrs. Smith said checking her dainty wrist watch.

"Wonderful. I too have registered for the game. How many participants, Mrs. Smith?" Ella queried.

"That's wonderful! Mr. Smith wrote down your name in the register, I guess. Let me see," Mrs. Smith said checking the register lying on the table before her. "There are thirty participants in all, dear. You'll be sitting at table number twelve. Here's your badge."

"Thank you, Mrs. Smith. Has my partner come in? Who is it? Anyone I know?" Ella queried eagerly.

"Let me see, dear. He's a fine young gentleman... such good manners... now what's his name..." Mrs. Smith turned a page of her register only to be interrupted.

"... Mrs. Smith... Mrs. Smith... Please hurry and come with me. Mr. Smith is calling you. He can't find the rope for the tug of war that's about to begin," a young girl named Margaret rushed to the table out of breath.

"O dear! It was in that big bag in which the spoons were kept with the lemons. Margaret, come with me. But then, who'll sit here at the registration desk?" Mrs. Smith looked worried.

"Shall I?" Ella offered.

"Mrs. Smith, Mr. Smith has sent me to take over the registration desk from you. He's calling you urgently," a young boy appeared just then.

"Thank you, Scott. Please see that the game of scrabble begins on time. All the participants have almost reached. Ella, could you please help him and then join your partner for the game?" Mrs. Smith said hurrying away.

"Yes, Mrs. Smith. You don't worry," Ella said.

~

"Table twelve... Ah... There it is," Ella mumbled as she walked to the place allotted to her.

Ella nodded and smiled at several people she knew from her town and also the neighbouring towns. Some were strangers but were happy to wave or nod in a friendly manner at this pleasant looking girl.

She finally reached her table and stopped short.

"You! Not again..." she groaned closing her eyes and shaking her head.

"Yes, me. Good afternoon Miss Wilson," Andrew stood up and drew out her chair opposite to his. "Please sit down. I guess the game is about to begin in a few minutes."

"O God! I wonder why you keep turning up everywhere I go!" grumbled Ella sitting down.

"Looks like destiny wants us to keep meeting," smiled Andrew and took up his place at the table again.

"I didn't know that you play scrabble. Let me warn you I'm good at this game and my opponent rarely wins," Ella said fixing him with a stare.

"Good to know that Miss Wilson, I'll bear that in mind. I'm flattered to be playing with a dangerous adversary. It'll give my rusted brains some good exercise," Andrew smiled charmingly.

"What's got into you since morning? You're being the perfect gentleman," Ella looked at him suspiciously.

Andrew laughed. She looked at him in amazement. For some curious reason she thought she'd like to hear him laugh again. It had a pleasant quality about it.

Just then the young boy Scott began reading the rules. And, then the participants started pitching their wits against each other trying to come up with words that could get them the most points.

"S-I-L-E-N-C-E"

"Good word, Miss Wilson. It can be pressing at times though. I would like to say P-E-A-C-E is better," Andrew placed the letters on the board.

"Great, Mr. Anderson. It's a matter of our C-H-O-I-C-E. What you think?" Ella looked at him and cocked a dainty eyebrow.

"A-G-R-E-E-D, my fair lady," smiled Andrew and bowed as he made his word.

Ella laughed aloud. She was enjoying herself, more than she had expected. Andrew wasn't that bad she thought.

Time flew on wings and they were twenty minutes into the game with ten still remaining. They both were lost in making words, explaining, giving examples... completely impervious to the voices around them of other players at nearby tables.

"A-N-A-M-C-A-R-A"

"What's that word, Mr. Anderson?" Ella frowned, looking up at him. "Is that a word? Or are you making it up? I've never heard of it."

"It's very much a word, Miss Wilson. I'm surprised you've never heard of it," Andrew said looking at her seriously.

"Really? What does it mean, may I ask?" Ella folded her arms and looked at him curiously.

"Anam Cara means 'soul friend'. It's an old Gaelic word. In ancient Celtic tradition there's a divine understanding of love and friendship. What is fascinating is the concept of soul love. Anam means soul and Cara means friend. We all need an anam cara, that's what we all crave for as human beings, a soul friend. An anam cara loves you, understands you. You don't need to hide behind a mask and there's no need for pretence. You can be really just as you are because love allows understanding to blossom. And, understanding is priceless because when you feel you are understood you feel at home. With your anam cara you can create something eternal," Andrew said softly, his eyes holding hers.

She looked at him hardly daring to breathe. There was something that seemed to draw her to him; she could feel... she felt light headed. Her breath came in soft gasps as if she had been running. She could hear her heartbeats thundering in her ears. He seemed to be close, so close... Mesmerized she continued to gaze into his eyes, not moving, unaware of the time passing.

Suddenly there was a flash of lightening and loud rumble of thunder. Unwilling to, but with a start she looked away and out of the tent they sat in. It was raining!

"It's raining," she said loudly.

"Yes, it's raining," Andrew repeated dragging his gaze from her flushed face to look out.

"I've got to go," Ella said standing up hurriedly. "Hannah will be alone."

"Miss Wilson, it's pouring and the wind is roaring like crazy. I don't think this is a good idea. You may hurt yourself," Andrew stood up too.

"Mr. Anderson, this is probably nothing more than a freak storm. I've lived here all my life and I know these grounds like the back of my hand. You need not concern yourself on account of me. I'll be fine," Ella said walking to the opening of the tent. She slipped off her sandals and held them by their straps.

"Miss Wilson, I wouldn't do this… Seriously!" Andrew tried to dissuade her.

"Mr. Anderson, I'm going to do this. Hannah is alone. Moreover, did I tell you I love the rain?" she turned to look at him, her eyes sparkling with joy and face shining.

He couldn't help but stare at her in admiration.

"Very well, I'm coming with you then. I can't stand by and allow you to rush headlong into the storm," Andrew said with determination.

"Suit yourself, Mr. Anderson. I'll race you to my stall," Ella laughed and took off nimbly like a deer through the rain that had begun to slow down.

8

"Ella... Andrew... Why are you running around in the rain?" Hannah looked at them in astonishment as they dashed into the tent.

"I win..." laughed Ella.

"Yes, you win!" laughed Andrew.

"Ella... you both are soaking wet. What were you thinking of?" Hannah said sternly.

"Of you, Hannah," they chorused and then laughed again.

"Really!"

"Really... It came down pouring and I couldn't help but think that you would have to manage alone. All our confectionaries were placed out due to the customers we were expecting. Are you alright?" Ella asked sobering down and looking around.

"I'm perfectly alright, dear, and so are the cakes and cupcakes and sandwiches. Mrs. Hendricks son came and helped to put things away safely."

Hannah and Ella turned to look at the Hendricks who sat in their stall. Ella smiled and waved to the mother and son who waved back.

"I must go and thank Danny," Ella said and then sneezed.

"You'll catch your death of a cold! You're dripping wet," Hannah gently rebuked Ella. "You shouldn't have run through the rain like this. What do you say, Andrew?"

Andrew looked at Ella standing before him, bare feet and her clothes dripping rain water onto the dry carpet inside the stall's tent. Her long dark brown hair stuck to her. The white lacy blouse quite transparent now, was plastered to her skin. The soaked pretty leaf green skirt moulded the slender curves of her hips and thighs. He felt a sensation he had not felt in long. His eyes flew to her lips and eyes before he looked away hurriedly.

"It was the need of the moment, I guess," Andrew said and shrugged.

"Here... take these hand towels, both of you and wipe your hair. I'm going to call up to Peggy and you're to go to her immediately. You need to change out of those clothes. Where's my cell phone?" Hannah said turning away.

"Who's Peggy?" queried Andrew wiping his hair vigorously.

"She's the in-charge of the linen and laundry in the castle, in fact, has been since years. Her ancestors have served Lord Whitman's family since ages," Ella supplied, smiling at him through the curtain of her hair.

"Ohh..." Andrew managed. He couldn't stop staring at her face framed by the dark locks. For a moment he had a vision of her hair fanned about her beautiful face on his pillow. He closed his eyes and counted to ten.

"Are you alright?" Ella asked in concern.

His eyes flew open. "Yes, yes. I'm fine. I think I should go," He said placing the towel on a chair.

"Andrew, you and Ella are to go this very minute to Peggy. She's waiting for you both inside the castle," Hannah who had been speaking on the phone now turned to them with a stern look on her face. "Just imagine! Adults behaving like kids!"

"No need to worry about me, Hannah. I'll be fine. I'll go back to where I'm staying and change," Andrew said with a smile which faltered when he saw Hannah place her hands on her hips. "Alright... Where do we have to go?"

Ella giggled and said, "Come with me."

"Ok..." Andrew said meekly and followed her out.

~

"Hannah is quite a dragon when she gets into one of her moods," Ella said as they walked down a corridor.

"Yes, I'm glad she didn't breathe fire. On the contrary, if she did, we would have got dry out there instead of having to come here," Andrew said following Ella.

Ella laughed and then stopped before a door. "Here's the room where Peggy works."

She knocked at a door.

"Come in," called a cheerful voice.

Ella pushed open the old, wooden door, polished beautifully.

"Hello Peggy," Ella said.

"Hello dear. So nice to see you. It's been a while since you visited us," Peggy rose from the chair she had been sitting in and came towards them.

"Yes Peggy. The tourist season is always so busy," Ella said hugging her. "How have you been?"

"I'm good as you can see. I'd been missing those chicken sandwiches from your cafe. I sent my husband to get some for me today from your stall. They were delicious as always. I'm afraid you'll think me to be greedy but I couldn't resist them. I had three," laughed the older woman.

"No... I wouldn't think that of you. I'd rather say you're a loyal customer who thinks highly of our wares," laughed Ella.

"O dear! I'm so sorry I didn't notice your young man. How rude of me!" Peggy said as she suddenly realized they had company.

"Oh... Sorry Peggy. I forgot to introduce my 'friend'. This is Andrew Anderson. He's a photographer. He's here to click pictures for a forthcoming exhibition he has in the big city. And, this is Peggy Priestman. Her family has served this household for ages," Ella said putting an arm around the short and stout lady's shoulders.

"Hello Mrs. Priestman. I'm so glad to meet you," Andrew shook her hand warmly.

"Hello dear. Oh my... you're all wet... the both of you. I almost forgot why Hannah sent you here. You must change your clothes. I've taken out a set for each of you." Peggy said, walked to a cupboard and opened it.

Andrew looked around the room with interest. It was covered from floor to ceiling with wooden panelling that cleverly hid cupboards which contained endless linens and upholstery items.

"Here... a lady's outfit and a gent's outfit," Peggy handed them the clothes and pointed towards a door in the corner of the circular room. "You can go through that narrow door and change in the restroom."

"Thank you, Peggy," Ella said leading the way.

"Oh hush! Don't embarrass me. Change and give me your things I'll have them dried out in a jiffy," Peggy said with a smile.

Andrew somehow reached the door before her and held it open for Ella. She looked at him in surprise but passed him to enter the passage beyond.

There was a washing room where laundry must've been washed when the family lived here and opposite it was a small restroom with all the modern fittings of wash basin, taps and toilet.

"You change first," said Andrew placing his clothes on a tiled counter. "I'll wait here."

"Are you sure?" asked Ella looking at him in surprise. "Your shoes must be squelchy."

"I'll deal with those out here while you change," he insisted.

"Ok. I hope Peggy has some slippers or footwear for us," Ella said stepping into the room and shutting the door.

~

"What a relief!" Ella said as she stepped out of the restroom after a couple of minutes holding her damp clothes. "I'll give these to Peggy."

She stopped short and stared at Andrew's bare back and trim waist. He had taken off his soggy shirt and was wiping his chest with the towel. The muscles in his arms and back rippled as he moved. He turned around when he heard her and she drew in a shaky breath.

In turn, he took in her appearance. Dressed in a simple blue cotton frock patterned with pink and white flowers and her long hair falling loosely over her shoulders she looked delightful.

"Ahem... I got us both a pair of slippers from Peggy while you were changing. This one's for you."

He pointed to a pair on the floor.

"Ok... thank you," she said and continued to stand before the door and stare at the slippers.

"Miss Wilson... May I?" Andrew finally said.

"Oh... yes... yes... I'm sorry," Ella stammered as she stepped aside for him.

She hurried back to Peggy, quite red in the face as she heard the door to the restroom close. Why was she feeling so hot, she wondered. Had summer already come?

"This portrait is of the late Lord Whitman. He looks so handsome, doesn't he?" Ella said looking at the huge portrait that hung over the mantelpiece in the reception hall.

"Hmm... He does. This is a beautiful room," Andrew looked around appreciatively.

"Isn't it? You'll find that this entire castle is awesome. I've been coming here as a child. And, I often imagined living here, surrounded by all this beautiful stuff and history. Come, I'll show you the ball room also called the banquet hall, and the dining room. They're majestic," Ella said excitedly.

"I can't wait. Let's go," Andrew smiled at the eager face before him and followed her, their feet hardly making a sound on the carpeted floor.

"See... This is the ball room. Isn't it fabulous?" Ella walked through the wide open mahogany doors into a magnificent room with large French windows covered with chintz curtains. A splendid chandelier hung overhead.

"It definitely is," Andrew agreed. "I like the view from these French windows too."

"Ohh... Yes, they're interesting. These French windows open to a marble porch or balcony as you can see. The steps of the balcony lead down into a lovely garden of blooming roses and sparkling fountains. It's a private garden, called the Rose Garden. It is said that the last Lord Whitman had courted his bride there and proposed marriage to her. Romantic, isn't it?" Ella's eyes sparkled as she spoke.

"Very...! Miss Wilson, I must say you look quite charming in that cotton dress," Andrew said without thinking.

"Why! Thank you, Mr. Anderson. If you're trying to charm me, it's not going to work. I've not yet forgotten how you hurt my feelings yesterday," laughed Ella, realising suddenly that yesterday seemed ages ago.

"Oh... In that case, I must try harder to earn my forgiveness," Andrew said with a bow.

"It's ok. You too look good in the cotton shirt, trousers and breeches. I guess what the people wore long back did make them stand out," smiled Ella, trying to be practical.

"May be..." agreed Andrew. "How about having a look at the dining room?"

He couldn't bear to look at her standing framed in the French windows surrounded by the white curtains and not want to do something he felt she would never forgive him for. He turned and walked away.

~

"The dining hall was exceptionally magnificent, Miss Wilson and, the library so extensive. I'm impressed," Andrew said.

"Wait till you see the study. It's even better," Ella put her hand on the beautifully carved doors before them.

"Allow me," said Andrew and pushed open the heavy wooden doors. "After you."

Ella smiled at him and entered the room that smelled of beeswax and leather.

"Hmm... Quite a masculine room! I like the leather upholstery, and the table is incredible. This must be truly archaic. Isn't it? The table, I mean," Andrew looked at Ella.

"Yes, I remember my father telling me, its 17th century something," Ella said with pride in her voice.

Andrew paused to look at her thoughtfully.

"You do know this place like the back of your hand," Andrew said impressed.

"No, there are still many things I don't know, like about the dagger kept in the showcase. I mean... I know that it's archaic too, from the 17th century again. But I've no idea about opening the showcase without setting off the alarm," laughed Ella.

"What do you mean?" enquired Andrew.

"That dagger is priceless. Come, let's have a look at it," Ella said as she led him to a smaller table covered with a glass top.

On a royal blue velvet cushion lay a dagger encrusted with pigeon egg sized rubies and emeralds.

"This dagger was a wedding gift by the emperor to Lord Whitman's great grandfather on his marriage to the emperor's niece," Ella said staring at the artefact.

"Interesting! I'm sure there must be many people who are after it, trying to lay their hands on this extraordinary artefact. How hasn't it been stolen till date?" Andrew asked peering at it with interest.

"There have been attempts to steal it but no one has been successful. For one, the security system is quite strong. Second, not everyone is allowed into this study," Ella said looking at him.

"Then, how did we get in?" asked Andrew curiously.

"Mr. Anderson, we're in the old wing of the castle that is not open to the public. Had you been a mere tourist on your own, you would have not reached here. Tell me, have you not realized that we're walking around corridors and looking into rooms, but have seen no one except ourselves reflected in mirrors?" Ella turned her head to one side and looked at him with raised eyebrows.

Andrew blinked in surprise.

"You're right. I'm sorry but I failed to realize that. I guess I was too taken up by the magnificence and history of this place and also the charming company," Andrew conceded.

"You see, I'm from the local people. Everyone working here knew my father. He visited this place often; he was a scholar of history and was studying this place, using the books in the library. He wanted to pen a book on the history and legends of the Whitman Castle," Ella said plainly. "And, I came here with him on many of those visits. Those people still serve in this castle and know me."

"Ah... I got it. So, if anyone wanted to steal this dagger, they would have to make friends with you to get in here first," Andrew said seriously.

"Mr. Anderson, I hope that's a joke," Ella squeaked and looked at him in alarm.

"Yes, it is nothing but a joke," laughed Andrew. "But believe me it's quite a tempting prospect. This dagger must be worth millions."

"I'm sure Peggy must've dried out our clothes. Let's go," Ella said in a voice that showed her discomfort.

"Yes. Let's go," Andrew said. He stopped beside the table for one last long look at the dagger.

"Mr. Anderson... Are you coming?" Ella called urgently.

"Yes... coming!" Andrew said, finally following her out of the room.

Ella looked at him strangely.

"Mr. Anderson, I must tell you again that it's impossible to enter this wing of the castle," Ella said walking in front of her companion.

"Miss Wilson, I've got your point. I won't try to enter this wing of the castle or rob the dagger," said Andrew.

Ella gasped, stopped and turned around.

"I didn't say that," Ella whispered in a shocked tone.

"No, you didn't but you did imply it by trying to warn me," Andrew said looking at her calmly.

"Very well, because you did sound as if you wanted to, Mr. Anderson. You can't blame me for it," Ella said heatedly.

"No, I'm not blaming you at all," Andrew said.

"Good..." Ella said turning away.

"Now that we've been around the private wings of the castle, you've begun to think I'm not that bad... Why do you still insist on calling me Mr. Anderson?" Andrew asked walking beside her.

"Isn't that your name?" she queried.

"No..."

"No?" she looked at him sideways.

"I mean, my name is Andrew. Why not call me 'Andrew'?" he asked.

"Mr. Anderson, sounds better," Ella insisted.

"Whatever, suit yourself!" Andrew shrugged and then added urgently. "Watch out!"

He grabbed her arm and pulled her to him as two men dressed in their livery walked through the narrow corridor carrying a heavy table.

"Sorry Miss Ella, can't stop. Are you alright?" called one, looking back as he continued to walk with the load.

"No problem," croaked Ella, all the breath knocked out of her.

She sighed and rested her forehead on his chest, aware only of her escalated heartbeats.

Once those began to calm down, she breathed deeply and inhaled his after shave. She now became aware of his arms around her waist still holding her to him, her fingers felt the muscles on his chest flex and she swallowed hard. An image of him standing shirtless before her flashed in her mind's eye.

She drew back hurriedly, not daring to look at him.

"Peggy must be wondering where we've gone," she said nervously, almost running down the corridor.

"Indeed!" She heard him say seriously which sounded suspiciously as if he was laughing at her.

He followed her through the corridor and into Peggy's work station without a word but with a gleam in his eye as if he was amused about something.

Someone rang the doorbell and Ella called out, "Coming..."

She opened the door and was surprised to see a stranger standing before her.

"Good evening, dear. My name is Lucia," said the kind looking old lady.

"Good evening. I'm sorry... I don't recognise you. Is there something I can do to help you?" queried Ella.

"I'm your new neighbour, dear. I've just moved in today afternoon," the lady said with a smile.

"Today afternoon?"

"Yes dear, you heard the thunder and saw the lightning? That's exactly when I arrived. It was raining cats and dogs. I hate arriving any place like that. But it always happens... I can't help it," the lady said shrugging her shoulders.

"Oh... You've moved in into the house across the road? How wonderful! It's been closed for over a year now," Ella smiled warmly, still trying to make sense of what the old woman was saying.

"Yes dear. It's a beautiful house but it's been closed a while so..." Lucia said and let her words trail away.

"Why don't you come in for a cup of tea? I'm sure you must be tired and thirsty," Ella offered kindly.

"Thank you, dear. You're so generous. I've been busy all afternoon and evening. It's almost eight now. I saw the light in your house burning and thought I should come and meet one neighbour at least," Lucia said following Ella into her kitchen.

"I hope you won't mind sitting here. Or would you like to sit in the living room?" Ella asked putting the kettle on to boil.

"No... No... I love the kitchen. It's such a warm place to be, it's a place where love can be cooked and served," Lucia smiled as she watched Ella move around setting the tray.

"Please do sit down... What shall I call you?" Ella looked up from slicing a plum cake.

"Mrs. Merryweather. Lucia Merryweather, that's my name," Lucia said making herself comfortable in a chair at the kitchen table. "Even though the weather's hardly merry when I arrive."

Ella laughed politely.

"You have such a beautiful kitchen, dear. It's so warm and welcoming," Mrs. Merryweather said looking around appreciatively.

"Thank you, Mrs. Merryweather. Are you alone or your family is here with you? I could pack a small hamper for all of you," Ella said thoughtfully.

"No need for that, dear. A cup of tea would be more than enough. I'm alone at the moment. I expect company in a day or two," Lucia said with a twinkle in her eye which Ella missed as she turned to get the cups and saucers.

"Mrs. Merryweather, in that case would you care to join me for dinner? I'm alone too. We could keep each other company. The food tastes better when you have someone to share it with," Ella said carrying the tray carefully to the table.

"My dear, you're taking too much of trouble. I wouldn't dream of putting you to an inconvenience," Lucia said taking the cup of tea Ella offered her.

"No trouble at all, Mrs. Merryweather. I was going to have a cold supper. There's a green salad, chicken roast and some bread with cheese. What do you say?" Ella asked sitting down opposite her with a cup of tea.

"Hmm... It sounds delicious to me. I've suddenly realised how famished I am," Lucia grinned with the innocence of a five-year old. "It's been years that I tasted a good chicken roast."

"In that case, let's finish the tea and I'll serve the meal. We can have this cake as dessert with home-made strawberry ice-cream," Ella said enthusiastically.

"I feel like a little girl at a birthday party. And, I've not had ice-cream in quite a while now," Lucia said with an excitement in her voice.

"Great!" laughed Ella looking at her curiously.

~

"This meal is just awesome," Mrs. Merryweather said putting down her fork and knife.

"I'm glad you liked it," Ella said sitting back and smiling at this lady she had taken a liking for, however eccentric.

"I'm not surprised that your cafe is doing so well. I must come there someday," Lucia said taking a sip from her glass of water.

"Why not tomorrow?" Ella said eagerly.

Lucia laughed at her enthusiasm. "I would have loved to but I've got to see to a few things in my house. Probably in a day or two I'll visit your cafe."

"Do you need any help? Shall I come over to your place early tomorrow morning to help? I could visit again later in the evening. I'll get you some soup, toast and mince pie for supper," Ella offered.

"Thank you, dear girl. You're so kind. But don't worry I have spoken to an agency they'll send someone over to help organize the house. I want to be around whilst they're there," Mrs. Merryweather said.

"Ah... yes. I understand. Mrs. Merryweather, you could visit the Whitman Castle. We're currently having the Spring Fair. And, it's not very far from here, just a walking distance of ten to fifteen minutes. You could finish your work and join me at my stall for tea in the late afternoon," suggested Ella. "Moreover, Hannah would love to meet you."

"Hannah? Oh... yes. I remember, the lady who's been your support after your dear parents passed on. I remember you just told me," said Mrs. Merryweather taking another sip of water.

"Yes, Hannah is a real darling and my greatest support," Ella smiled warmly.

"How nice! You're such a lovely, talented and warm girl... I can't help but wonder why no young man has pledged his love to you," Mrs. Merryweather said thoughtfully.

"No idea! I'll get the dessert," Ella rose from the table laughing.

"Did you make the ice-cream too?" queried Lucia following her to the sink to keep her plate.

"No... Not today. I try my hand at it when I have some time but these days I'm busy at the Fair," Ella said scooping ice-cream generously on to a thick slice of plum cake.

"This smells heavenly and tastes divine," Mrs. Merryweather sniffed appreciatively and then tasted some.

"Thank you," smiled Ella eating from her bowl.

"This is how love should be... mushy and sweet. What do you think, dear?" Lucia said raising another spoonful to her mouth.

"Maybe... I've no idea about that," Ella said with a small smile.

"Well, love can be annoying and disturbing too. It can make you all hot and bothered. I sometimes feel that the right kind of love can make a woman purr like a cat but give her the wrong attitude and she can roar like a lioness. And, believe me no man can handle that version of her. It's terrifying!" Lucia said with a twinkle in her eye.

"Wow! What a way to put that!" Ella laughed loudly. "I love that description. It sounds quite interesting."

"It does. Doesn't it?" Lucia said keeping the bowl in the sink. "And, now I better make a move. I'll leave you to dream of the one who makes you want to roar."

"There's no one, Mrs. Merryweather," insisted Ella and laughed.

"Very well. Then there must be someone who makes you want to purr..." Lucia looked at Ella slyly and said softly. "Someone... who makes your heart race... your nerves flutter... Someone who makes you feel weak in your knees... the thought of who gives you butterflies..."

Ella drew in a sharp breath and tried to dismiss the memory of a familiar face... shirtless, bare feet, hair damp from the rain.

Lucia staring at her face smiled. Her god daughter seemed to be on the threshold of love. The attraction was surely there. It was going to be fun to give her and that Andrew a little push towards each other. She felt a fountain of joy welling up in her heart. Her god daughter would surely have her very own love story. Now, where was that Andrew?

11

"So finally you have a new neighbour," Hannah said handing over a doughnut to a customer.

"Yes."

"What did you say her name was?" queried Hannah wiping her hands.

"Mrs. Merryweather. She arrived yesterday afternoon when the storm was raging," Ella said placing more doughnuts on the empty tray.

"Ah... By the way Andrew called up to me to say that he would come by sometime today to thank you for yesterday's tour of the castle," Hannah supplied, looking at Ella eagerly. "You didn't tell me about that."

"Well... There wasn't anything to tell in that. I just took him around while Peggy dried out our things. I showed him the ballroom, the study and all. It was nothing," Ella said quickly.

"It was the part of the castle where only known people are allowed. And, you took 'him' there. You defend the privacy of the place just like your father did," Hannah said.

"Yes. Yes, but how else could we have spent that time? No big deal Hannah. He's not dangerous, is he?" Ella said and then remembered something with a twinge of guilt.

"What?" asked Hannah looking at her face.

"What?" repeated Ella.

"You thought of something. Your expression changed," Hannah said with concern. "What's troubling you?"

"Nothing, Hannah. I'm fine," Ella smiled reassuringly.

"Are you sure?"

"Yes. Yes, of course, Hannah."

"Hello there!" called a voice.

Ella and Hannah turned to see who it was.

"Hello Mrs. Merryweather. How nice to see you!" Ella said, a smile lighting up her face.

"Hello dear. I'm so happy to meet you... and Hannah," Lucia beamed at both the ladies.

"Hello Mrs. Merryweather. I'm glad to meet you. Ella was just telling me about you," Hannah said smiling at the old lady with silver hair who looked nothing less than eighty.

"Was she now? I hope she wasn't praising me too much. It gets a little embarrassing for an old woman like me to have many admirers," Mrs. Merryweather chuckled.

"O My God! I was just doing that," laughed Ella.

"Mrs. Merryweather, please come. Would you care to have some lemonade?" Hannah offered. "You must be thirsty."

"Oh... That would be lovely. It's so warm today. Who'll say it rained yesterday?" Lucia said sitting down on a chair Ella offered her.

"Yesterday's storm was truly unexpected. It blew up suddenly," Hannah said filling a paper glass with the refreshing drink.

"Just like love, it sneaks up on you suddenly, when you least expect it," Lucia took the glass Hannah held out to her and took a grateful sip.

"True..." Hannah whispered and looked at the older woman thoughtfully. This woman was strange.

"Did you go around the grounds, Mrs. Merryweather? They're magnificent at this time of the year. The rose bushes are teeming with fragrant blossoms. Then, there are daffodils and daisies too. It's a real riot of colours all around. I sometimes wonder how do the bees and butterflies decide which flowers to choose? You must see them, they're a feast for the eyes," Ella said as she waved goodbye to one of the children who bought a muffin.

"No, my dear. I've just come. I'll go around once I catch my breath. I'm sure the place will be even more beautiful by the time Easter comes," Mrs. Merryweather said.

"Yes, Yes. It will be Easter in two weeks," said Hannah. "That's the day the Spring Festival closes with a grand celebration. There'll be the usual church service and then everyone will gather in the church grounds for a community breakfast and come here for the vintage car rally. Prizes for the best maintained car and also the oldest working model will be announced among other prizes in the late afternoon."

"Wow! I never knew that," Ella said with interest.

"The sheriff told me yesterday afternoon when he came for the daily rounds. And, yes, he also mentioned that we need to beware of a few crooks that are going about disguised as gentle folk. In fact, now that we're talking, I remember he also mentioned a gang of noted thieves are here with malicious intents," Hannah said.

"What malicious intent, Hannah?" Ella asked curiously.

"They wish to get hold of valuable stuff from inside the castle too. The sheriff said that we were to report any suspicious people or actions. He said we need to be extra vigilant," Hannah said.

"What? Oh no!" squeaked Ella alarmed.

"What happened, Ella?" Hannah asked.

"Nothing... Nothing..." Ella said a little breathlessly. "It's... It's... just scary."

"So much like love... It's scary to think someone will steal your heart someday. That crazy thing will belong to you but it will beat for someone else, it will quicken when the object of your affection comes before your eyes," Mrs. Merryweather said dreamily.

Hannah and Ella looked at the older woman sipping from her paper cup.

"Hello everyone," Andrew said just then.

"Andrew... How nice to see you!" Hannah said happily.

"Hello..." Ella breathed aware of her heart beating erratically. She looked at Mrs. Merryweather smiling at her and smiled back feebly.

"Hello young man! And, who may you be? A suitor for dear Ella? A prince charming?" Mrs. Merryweather said looking him over.

"Mrs. Merryweather, this is Andrew Anderson. He's a professional photographer. He's here to take pictures of the Spring Fair and our quaint little town. He'll be having an exhibition soon in the big city in some part of the world. And, Andrew... this is Mrs. Merryweather... she's..."

"Hello Andrew! It's wonderful to meet a few good young men today, dressed decently with a proper haircut and a clean shaven face. I intend to take a walk around the grounds of this castle. I don't want to disturb this beautiful girl Ella and her devoted friend Hannah. They're busy serving their customers. Do you think you'll be able to take me around and show me some interesting sights? Eh?" Mrs. Merryweather asked pertinently.

Andrew looked taken aback just momentarily and then his half smile was back in place. He said, "Why not? It would be a pleasure, ma'am. May I offer you my arm for you to lean on?"

"You do know your manners. And, you sound as good as you look. Let's see how long you'll hold on to that image," Mrs. Merryweather said looking at him with her bright eyes.

"I hope I'll not disappoint you," Andrew bowed his head courteously and offered his arm. "Shall we go around the castle grounds, ma'am?"

"Very well. Let's do it. I feel I'm going to enjoy your company. We can have a nice little chat as we go around and you can tell me about yourself," Mrs. Merryweather said standing up and taking his arm. "I'll see you later, Ella dear and Hannah."

"Goodbye Hannah! See you later Miss Wilson," Andrew nodded as he sauntered off with the old lady.

Ella watched him bend his head towards her neighbour as he listened to something she said and laugh. He towered over the older woman who was short and plump.

"A nice young fellow, I've always said. He's always so courteous and jolly. I don't know why you don't like him," Hannah said looking at her sideways.

"I've no idea why you would say that, Hannah. I don't understand what you mean?" Ella shrugged her shoulders as she folded a hand towel with exaggerated care.

"You very well know what I mean even if you don't want to accept it," Hannah said still watching the two figures walking among the crowd.

Ella followed her gaze and saw Andrew introducing Mrs. Lucia Merryweather to the Pastor who shook hands with her and clapped Andrew on the shoulder like an old friend.

'Strange!' She thought. 'Everyone seems to get on so well with him. Why do sparks fly only when I'm with him? Is he what he portrays who he is... or is he hiding something...? Is it that I can sense something is not fitting here...?' Her mind flew back to the conversation in the study.

Ella looked again at him as they disappeared behind a few stalls in the distance.

"Good morning, Ella. How are you, dear?"

"Good morning, Mrs. Merryweather. I'm good. Only a faucet in the kitchen isn't well. Horrible leak," Ella laughed into her phone.

"Ohh... Did you call the plumber?"

"I did. But Max is elsewhere and it will take him two hours to be here. No idea how it started. Everything was fine moments ago. I used it today morning when I washed the coffee mug," Ella looked at the dripping tap. "I've got to leave in an hour to go to the castle."

"No worries, dear. I'll send my paying guest. He'll be more than willing to help," Mrs. Merryweather said with a tinkle in her voice.

"You have a paying guest?"

"Yes, didn't I tell you?"

"Not that I can remember you mentioning it.'

"I'm an old lady. I must've forgotten, dear. He'll be along in a jiffy."

"You sound ..." Ella said, not quite sure how to put it.

"Happy, excited...?" queried Mrs. Merryweather.

"Well... yes. Sort of," Ella said biting her lip.

"Why shouldn't I be?" Mrs. Merryweather said.

"Sorry...?"

"I mean, my dear, you've been of great help to me this last week. I'm happy I can do something for you," Mrs. Merryweather said quickly. "I'll just send him over to your place. Goodbye."

"Bye. Take care," Ella said disconnecting the call and looking at the screen thoughtfully. "Strange!"

~

"Yes! Please come to the back door. I'm in the kitchen," called Ella loudly, when she heard a knock on the front door.

The radio station was playing 'Can't Help Falling in Love' and Ella sang along softly.

Within minutes she heard footsteps and someone knocked.

"Please come in," Ella called, her hands covered in flour.

She looked up when the door opened and a tall figure entered into her beautifully kept kitchen. Her eyes widened in surprise.

"You? What are you doing here?"

"I. Yes, me. I'm here to help you," Andrew said with a faint smile. He registered the song playing and raised his eyebrows questioningly.

"You're here to help me, with what?" asked Ella at a loss for words. She ignored his expression.

"Your kitchen's tap, I believe. Well, that's what Mrs. Merryweather told me," Andrew said looking around.

"You're Mrs. Merryweather's paying guest?" she asked incredulously. "Since when?"

"It's going to be a week if I remember correctly," he supplied.

"Really? Are you following me?" Ella queried suspiciously.

"Following you? For what?" Andrew asked in surprise.

"No idea..." Ella said hurriedly. "Do you know how to repair taps? I didn't think you looked that type."

"What is my type according to you, Miss Wilson?" Andrew asked arching an eyebrow.

"I'm no one to set you in any type. How am I to know? I mean I don't know you well..."

"Exactly! But you seem determined to think that I'm some dishonest kind of a guy."

"See... Mr. Anderson..." Ella hesitated.

"Yes, Miss Wilson. I'm here to *see* the leaking tap. So if you'll show me the cranky chap I'll treat him quickly and go before you get any more ideas of me following you and trying to... you know..." Andrew shrugged his shoulders.

"Very well. Here it is. It's this one," Ella pointed out the tap quickly.

"Great! Let me have a look at it," Andrew went over to the tap and tinkered with it.

"Are you sure you'll manage? Have you done something like this before?" Ella queried trying to peer over his shoulder.

"Hmm... I assure you, I have, Ma'am. Plenty of them," Andrew said working with a wrench.

Ella looked at his back doubtfully and then turned to the kitchen counter.

"I thought you were a photographer," Ella said covering the dough she had been kneading with a clean cotton cloth and keeping it aside.

"Yes, I'm a photographer but I'm pretty useful around the house too," Andrew said working on the tap.

"Really?" You don't look..." began Ella only to stop short when Andrew turned his head to look at her with raised eyebrows.

"I mean..."

"Yes, pray do tell me what do you mean, Miss Wilson," urged Andrew.

Ella didn't answer for a few seconds. She looked at the back of his head, and took a deep breath.

"The wing of the castle you... I mean we visited that day is completely off limits for the general public. It's secured with the best of systems and it's difficult to get away with anything from there," Ella said lamely.

"Point noted. I won't try anything hanky-panky there, if that's what you're implying," Andrew grunted as he worked single-mindedly with the tap. "Please, rest your mind on that."

"Mr. Anderson... I... I mean..." Ella wiped her hands on a kitchen towel. She walked closer to the sink and stood beside him.

"I know what you mean, Miss Wilson. You don't have a very good impression of me, I can see. But let me assure you that whatever you may think of me... I'm not a... Oh no!"

"What..." Ella had time to say before Andrew fumbled with the spanner and then grappled with a full flow of water wetting them both.

"I'm so sorry... Sorry..." Andrew said trying to stem the flow.

"What are you doing? My whole kitchen..." Ella said in exasperation, hurriedly placing her hands over his on the tap.

"I'll fix it. Just a moment," Andrew tried to fit the tap.

"Mr. Anderson..."

"There, that's done." Andrew said finally.

"Really? After you drenched my kitchen and me," Ella said looking at him with a frown.

He turned to look at her standing so close to him, her face and white blouse over her jeans dripping wet.

"Oh... I'm so, so sorry. I'm wet too," Andrew said. "Can I borrow a towel?"

Ella pursed her lips and looked at him as he wiped his face and ran his fingers through his dripping hair.

"Sure," she said as she walked out of the room.

"Wonderful! I wonder why it has to be me," grumbled Andrew under his breath.

"Here..." Ella returned within minutes with two towels. She handed him one and loosened the ribbon tying her dark curls.

Just then Elvis Presley chose to sing over the radio...

"Take the ribbon from your hair

Shake it loose and let it fall

Lay it soft upon on my skin

Like the shadows on the wall..."

Ella's eyes flew to Andrew. He was watching her with a strange look in his eyes. She felt that same old sensation she felt that day in the corridor of the castle when he held her close to his chest. She felt she had been running for miles and she struggled to breathe.

"O my dears! What happened? You both are soaking wet," Mrs. Merryweather said walking in through the kitchen door.

Mrs. Merryweather looked from one to the other and suppressed a smile.

"What happened?" she repeated, "This place looks a mess. There's water everywhere."

"Ahem... Nothing! There was a small accident with the tap," Andrew answered. "I think I better go. I'll need to change. The tap's repaired, Mrs. Merryweather."

"How wonderful, Andrew dear! You're such a helpful young man. So handy around the house too," Mrs. Merryweather said patting him on the arm as he passed her to leave. "Thank you."

"I'll be going out. I'll see you later in the evening, Mrs. Merryweather," Andrew said leaving.

"Yes, dear. I'll have supper ready for you," Mrs. Merryweather said waving.

~

"I'm so glad I came here with you this morning," Mrs. Merryweather said filling paper cups with lemonade.

“Thank you for accepting the invitation, Mrs. Merryweather,” Ella smiled warmly.

“Really, you’ve been a great help, Mrs. Merryweather. Just a week more to go for Easter, the holidays have begun. The crowds are getting larger,” Hannah said handing over a doughnut to a customer.

“Oh... it’s nothing! I enjoy opportunities to socialize. It’s so much fun!” Mrs. Merryweather said gleefully.

“Hello ladies!” said a male voice.

“Edward! What are you doing here? How have you been?” Ella said in surprise.

“Hello Ella! I’m glad you still remember me,” said the man. “Hello Hannah!”

“Hello Edward. It’s been a long time. Where have you been?” asked Hannah with distaste.

“I’ve been out in foreign parts of the world trying to set up my business. It’s just picking up. I’m so glad I could make it home for Easter,” he said.

“Great! Mrs. Merryweather, this is my childhood friend, Edward. We literally grew up together,” Ella introduced them. “And, this is Mrs. Merryweather, my new neighbour.”

“Hello young man, I wish I could say, nice to meet you but I don’t know you yet,” Mrs. Merryweather looked at him curiously.

“Hello Mrs. Merryweather. You look amazing. I’m sure you’ll get plenty of opportunities to meet me and know me better. I’ll be staying for a week at least and I’ll be visiting Ella often. There’s so much to catch up on,”

Edward said happily unaware of the looks Hannah was giving him.

"Most certainly, Edward. Have you met everyone? Sarah and James got married, and Kim had a baby girl just last month. Oh... there's so much to tell you," Ella said excitedly.

"I've not met anyone. I thought you'll take me around and fill me up with the latest news in the town. But I can see you're busy," Edward said sounding a little put out.

"No... no. I'm not that busy. Hannah will be able to manage for half an hour or so. I'll take you around to meet everyone and then we'll have some tea together," Ella said slipping off her apron and walking around the tables of her stall. "Hannah, you'll be fine?"

"No worries, Ella dear. We'll be fine, Mrs. Merryweather and I. You skip along and come back as quick as you can. We'll need you at tea-time," Hannah said. "Take care."

"Yes, I'll see you soon, Hannah. Come along, Edward," Ella said waving.

"This Edward guy, is he a good fellow?" Mrs. Merryweather asked looking at them talking to someone in the next stall.

"Sleazy fellow! I don't like him at all. He seems to be hiding something below the surface all the time. I don't know how Ella tolerates him," Hannah said cutting a slice from a cake with extra force.

"Hmm... I feel the same about him too. Looks like he's here for something," Mrs. Merryweather said thoughtfully. "I wonder what it is!"

"He's a good-for-nothing! God alone knows what business he's into. Ella has a clean heart and thinks everyone is as good as her. I only hope he disappears quickly," Hannah said.

"Amen to that!"

"Amen!" Hannah said fervently.

~

"I always love coming back home," Edward said taking a deep breath. "The fresh air, the greenery here is such a lovely change from the city."

"It's beautiful here in the Spring. It's always been. I love the blue skies, and how the ancient trees make a green tunnel at certain places on the streets and in lanes. The occasional rain adds to the sweet smell of flowers all around," Ella said inhaling deeply.

"So, how's life?" Edward asked.

"All good. The cafe is doing well," Ella said warmly.

"This Spring Fair will be ending soon?" Edward asked looking at the people walking around.

"Yes, Easter Sunday. There will be morning service in the church. The new Lord Whitman has invited the entire town and the other visitors to breakfast that day," Ella said waving to a small girl. "And, our cafe has been given the order to prepare the breakfast."

"Lord Whitman is here?" Edward looked at her sharply. "I mean... that's great news!"

“No... I’ve not heard he’s here,” Ella said with a frown. “Thanks.”

“Will he be coming then? This new Lord Whitman,” Edward queried.

“I don’t think so. I don’t think he can travel. He’s old and an invalid, I heard, but I’m not sure,” Ella said walking beside him.

“Hmm... So till what time do these grounds remain open to the crowds every day?” Edward asked.

“Six o’clock in the evening.”

“Is the castle open to the public like before?” Edward asked.

“Yes, of course. The new Lord Whitman was generous to agree to the earlier arrangements. In fact, there’s even a vintage car rally on Easter Sunday after the mass. Look there! Those are the vintage cars,” Ella said.

“Great! They look awesome. Looks like they’re drawing in the crowds too,” Edward said looking in the direction she was pointing.

“They’ll be driven out of the castle gates around the town and then back into the grounds. After that the prizes will be announced for these cars in different categories. Isn’t that awesome?” Ella said. “The media will be here. This will definitely boost the chances of business in the town. I’m sure more tourists will turn up in the coming months.”

“True! Now, how about you take me for a walk through the castle? It’s been years and years that I walked through the old corridors," Edward said, turning to smile at her.

"Just now? I..."

"Yes, come on, Ella. There aren't many people around just now. Hannah won't miss you. Besides, we may not get a chance to meet again here in the castle grounds," Edward wheedled her.

"Ok... let's go."

"Wonderful! Are the rooms just as before with those precious articles still around?"

"The rooms are more or less the same. But a few things have changed over the years. Not all the precious things are on display now, just the silver cutlery and bone china plates, cups and saucers," Ella said walking up the short flight of stairs to the magnificent entrance.

"Ohh... What about those diaries, coins, stamps, and swords?"

"Some are still there, others have been moved just like the dagger the emperor had gifted to the late Lord Whitman's great grandfather long back," Ella said.

"Why so?"

"Because there have been a few attempts to steal some of the archaic things from here," Ella said.

"No security, then?"

"No, cameras have been installed and other gadgets too... but..."

"So where have the things been shifted? I mean... it's scary to think these things are in danger of being lost,"

Edward asked gazing at a beautiful painting. "This was the previous Lord Whitman, wasn't he?"

"Yes, a very kind person. I met him a few times when I visited with Father. We used to often see him in the library. He loved books. He had many of the priceless things shifted to the library and study in recent years," Ella said.

"And, that's in the old part of the castle which no one is allowed to visit," Edward said. "How ingenious! I'm glad the antiques belonging to this castle and our town are safe. It's such a relief! Our future generations will be able to see those beautiful things which belonged to our glorious past. Come, let's have a look through those windows at the lake."

"Oh yes! I remember how we could see the lake shimmering in the afternoon sunshine from here. The view was and is still lovely. How I used to love running to and fro on that bridge!" Ella said happily, looking out from a window.

14

"Oh no!" Ella murmured and ran to take shelter under a tree.

Ella looked at the falling rain. She peeped through the dense leaves of the tree she had sheltered under in disbelief. Just a while ago the sky had been absolutely clear. From where did the clouds come? She was so busy puzzling over the change in weather that she didn't notice someone approaching with an umbrella.

"Miss Wilson...? What are you doing here?"

"Mr. Anderson? What are *you* doing here?"

"Mrs. Merryweather sent me to get some bread and eggs. I was on my way to Sam's shop when it came down pouring. I'm only grateful that Mrs. Merryweather insisted I carry an umbrella. The sky was a bright blue a couple of minutes back. Strange!" Andrew closed the umbrella and joined her under the tree.

"I was thinking on similar lines. It's really unexpected! I have bread and eggs with me. I just got them. No need to go all the way to Sam's place. I can lend you what you require at the moment," Ella said.

"Wonderful! Shall we go home then?"

"It's still raining!"

"We have an umbrella. It's quite large," Andrew offered.

"Ok. I think you're right. We've no idea how long it will rain. I'm hungry and thirsty as it is," Ella murmured.

"Alright then. Let's go home," Andrew said as he opened the umbrella.

~

Mrs. Lucia Merryweather smiled as she stirred the soup in her kitchen. "Hmm... it smells good. And, it's one of Ella's favourites. They'll be here soon."

"Mrs. Merryweather..." Andrew called.

"Come in through the kitchen door, dear. It's open!"

"What crazy weather! Miss Wilson, please come in," Andrew said pushing open the door.

"Ella... Andrew... Ohh..."

"Hello Mrs. Merryweather! I'm sorry for barging in just like this," Ella said brushing the raindrops from the skirt of her pink cotton dress.

"No trouble at all dear. You're wet. At least your feet are... These sandals are hardly any protection. Fancy, strappy things, even if they're tad comfortable for standing and walking all day they can't save your feet. Here take them off and wear those slippers. Andrew be a darling and fetch a towel for Ella," Mrs. Merryweather said, her eyes twinkling in delight. She hurried Ella further into the kitchen as Andrew left to do as she had instructed.

"Please don't worry, Mrs. Merryweather. I'm perfectly fine. I think I should go home. I'm just across the road," Ella said. "The floor is getting all damp."

"You're not going home just now. I won't allow it. And, never mind the floor. It can be mopped up. You go through that door. Andrew will give you a towel, go into the bathroom and tidy yourself," Mrs. Merryweather pushed her through the door and shut it firmly behind her with a happy smile.

She snapped her fingers. A mop rose into the air and began to wipe away the puddles of rainwater. She sang softly and stirred the soup again. She had time to prod the leg of mutton she had placed to roast in the oven before she heard footsteps again. She snapped her fingers and the mop hurried to its place in the corner of the room and stood still.

"Mrs. Merryweather, I couldn't reach Sam's place, it came down pouring. But Miss Wilson said she had eggs and bread..."

"No problem, Andrew dear. I understand. I just wanted to make an egg and bread pudding. Never mind we'll make one tomorrow," Mrs. Merryweather said.

"Why tomorrow? We'll make one now, I'll make it." Ella said walking into the kitchen.

"Ella, dear. You must be tired after the whole day. It's almost supper time," Mrs. Merryweather said.

"It won't take long, just half-an-hour," Ella said taking out eggs and the bread from her bag.

"Would you like to have a cup of tea, dear?" Mrs. Merryweather queried. "I just made some."

"O yes! That would be lovely. I'm so thirsty," Ella said. "Mrs. Merryweather please give me a large bowl and a whisk."

"Yes dear. Andrew, make yourself useful and help Ella with whatever she needs. I'm going to take my cup of tea and sit down for a while in the living room. My back isn't getting younger," Mrs. Merryweather poured three cups from a teapot that looked empty but apparently wasn't.

~

"Miss Wilson, is the milk sufficient?" Andrew asked pouring milk in a saucepan.

"Hmm... yes. Let it become lukewarm. Once it does, add it to the bowl of crushed bread. Where's the custard powder?"

"It's on that shelf, on your right," Andrew pointed with a spoon.

"This one? Found it. I'll require three teaspoons of it. Ok... Now I'll add some nutmeg, vanilla essence and the sugar. Mr. Anderson, I'm going to need two small bowls for the eggs."

"Wait a minute. I'll get them for you," Andrew said turning away from the gas stove. "They're here in this drawer."

"Mr. Anderson, the milk!" Ella said urgently as the milk raced to the top of the saucepan and threatened to boil over with a loud hissing sound.

"Oh no!"

They both collided in their rush to turn off the gas.

"Ouch! Mr. Anderson, you need to be a bit more careful," Ella said rubbing her arm.

"Do I? Sorry. Remember, you sent me to get the bowls for you," Andrew said showing her two bowls.

"But you could have turned the fire down," Ella said practically.

"I'm so sorry I never thought of it. You see, I don't spend much time with indisciplined entities that threaten to run when they're faced with a hot situation," Andrew said shrugging his shoulders.

"What?"

"Oh... Nothing! I think I was just trying to make up something funny!"

"Really? Had the milk over-boiled we would have had the funniest situation before us – to clean the mess," Ella pointed out. "Now, could you please help to crack these three eggs and separate the yolk from the whites?"

"Why not, Madam? With pleasure," Andrew bowed low and grinned at her.

"Here you go, Sire. Please add the yolks to this mixture here and whisk the whites," Ella instructed.

"It shall be done, Madam!" Andrew said carefully doing as he was told.

"Very good. Now, I'll add the milk and give this a good mix. Where's the pudding dish? Ahh... I'll just grease it with butter. There... that's done. In goes the blended mixture. Now, I'll place it in the oven and let it bake," Ella said working quickly.

Andrew watched her with a smile on his face as he continued to whisk the egg whites.

She shut the oven and turned around to see him looking at her.

"What?"

"What?" Andrew asked.

"Why are you staring at me like that?"

"Nothing... Nothing... Just that you've got a little powdered sugar on your temple," Andrew said placing the bowl on the kitchen counter and walking towards her.

"Where?" Ella asked trying to wipe it off.

"May I?" Andrew asked brushing off the granules just above her left eyebrow. He gazed deeply into her eyes and she stared at him frozen. His touch had started a flutter deep down in her chest. "Miss Wilson did anyone ever tell you, that you have beautiful eyes. Alive, mischievous, expressive... they seem to hold great secrets, and when you laugh they dance with mirth."

Andrew traced her eyebrow gently with his thumb, and then her left eye. She saw his face draw closer to hers before she shut her eyes in pleasure at his touch. He traced her left cheek, her lips and gently lifted her face to his. Her lips parted as she felt his breath feather her face and waited...

Andrew looked down at her face raised to his. Her skin was as delicate as the petals of a daisy and just as flawless. A tiny mole on her right cheek added to her beauty. Her lips parted and seemed to tremble, if he wasn't imagining it. He could smell her perfume, a gentle fragrance of roses.

'Ding!'

Ella opened her eyes. Her eyes widened suddenly and she drew away hastily.

"The timer has gone off. The pudding must be ready," Ella said.

Andrew searched her face and stepped back.

"Yes! The egg whites are stiff. You can use them," he said pushing the bowl towards her. "I'll go and see what Mrs. Merryweather is doing. Do you need me?"

Ella's hand stilled as she spread the whites over the pudding.

"I mean... Do you need any more help?" Andrew rephrased.

"No, no. Just tell Mrs. Merryweather the pudding will be done in ten minutes," Ella said as she placed the pudding once again in the oven.

"Ok. I'll do that," Andrew nodded as he stepped out and shut the door.

"O God!" Ella breathed and leaned against the kitchen counter. "What's wrong with me?"

~

"Ella dear, what aroma!"

"Thank you, Mrs. Merryweather. The pudding is done. All hot and golden brown," Ella placed the pudding dish on the counter and took off the gloves.

"Hmm... hmm... hmm... It smells delightful! You're a genius."

"I'm flattered, Mrs. Merryweather. Now, I must take your leave. The rain has stopped," Ella said placing the gloves beside the dish.

"No, I'm not going to hear of it. You're to stay to dinner. I've made your favourite peas soup and there's leg of mutton roast with mashed potatoes and this heavenly pudding. We can toast some bread and butter to go with it, what do you think?"

Ella smiled at the old lady standing in front of her. "I'm tempted!" she said plainly.

"Very good. Then, I'll lay the table there in the corner. Would you please call Andrew to dinner?"

"Me?" squeaked Ella.

"What happened?" Mrs. Merryweather looked at her in surprise.

"Nothing... I mean... I mean... I don't know..."

"He's in the living room watching some cricket match. Run along and tidy yourself in the bathroom under the stairs and then call him, girlie! Don't just stand there and look at me," Mrs. Merryweather hurried her. "It's already past my dinner time. And, I'm starving. Lord! Children nowadays are so fussy! Now go, dear."

"Yes, Mrs. Merryweather," Ella mumbled and hastened out.

All alone by herself, Mrs. Merryweather snapped her fingers and the table began to lay itself. A white cloth with lace edges spread itself over the shining wooden top. Drawers opened. Plates, glasses, spoons, forks, knives and other things flew in an organized manner and arranged themselves for three people. A bottle of red wine was the last to join the other things. A small centrepiece of spring flowers placed itself at the centre.

Mrs. Merryweather chuckled and rubbed her hands together. "This is fun! My dear goddaughter Ella, I can feel something stirring deep down in your heart and I'll do everything I can so that you can have your 'happily ever after'. Rains... eggs... bread... pudding... a dinner together. Anything! Oh... How I wish Andrew had kissed you this evening. Anyway... I'm loving this prelude to a delightful fairytale!"

~

"You cook so well, Mrs. Merryweather. The food is delicious," Ella said swallowing a morsel. "This roast is so juicy and tender."

"I'm glad you liked it. What about the soup?"

"Yes, that was yummy. I've never tasted such good peas soup before. You must share the recipe with me," Ella said.

"Andrew, you're pretty quiet. Isn't the meal to your liking, my dear?"

"No... I mean yes. It's delightful as always. I think I'm going to put on a lot of weight before I go back," Andrew said and laughed.

"What nonsense! You're young and young people need feeding up. And, what's this about going back?" Mrs. Merryweather asked surprised, pausing with her fork halfway to her mouth.

"Well, yes. I'll be leaving in a couple of days. I have that exhibition I need to look to. I have already outstayed the time I thought I would be here," Andrew said pushing around the peas on his plate.

"Well, that's disturbing. I thought you'd be here till things worked out..."

"What? What do you mean? What things have to work out?" Andrew looked at her curiously.

"The Spring Fair culminating... the vintage car rally ending... You know... You'll get good pictures of those too. I heard it's going to be a grand affair. And, it's just a matter of four or five days, Andrew. What's the point of leaving now?" Mrs. Merryweather cajoled him.

"My work is almost done here, Mrs. Merryweather. Just a day or two more and I'll be leaving. I must say I hate to do so but I can't help it..." Andrew reached across the table and squeezed her hand where it lay. "I'll miss you."

"Oh now come on! Don't get me all emotional. I know it in my old bones; you aren't going anyway till after Easter. No point discussing things which aren't happening," Mrs. Merryweather said brusquely, swatting away his hand. "Now let's eat up and then, Ella will serve the pudding."

"Yes Mrs. Merryweather," Andrew laughed. "I'm waiting to get a slice of the pudding too. I'm sure it's going to taste fantastic."

Ella looked at them talking happily and smiled wistfully. How lovely it would be to have… a family.

~

"Thank you and sorry for the trouble. You really didn't have to. I live just across the road," Ella said.

The moon shone brightly on the couple standing on the doorstep of the Wilson home. A silvery glow lit up the entire neighbourhood. A star spangled sky couldn't have looked prettier. Someone seemed to have scattered a million diamonds carelessly and each one of them shone brightly.

"The sky looks so beautiful tonight. Who'll say it rained all evening?" Ella whispered looking up. "Look at the moon, it's as pretty as a picture tonight."

"It is…" Andrew whispered.

Something in his voice made her look at him.

"Miss Wilson... Ella... I want to call you that," Andrew said softly, taking a step closer. "You look beautiful. You are beautiful. I wish..."

"You wish...?" Ella breathed mesmerized.

Andrew gazed into her eyes... Time seemed to have stilled.

Andrew closed his eyes. "Never mind! Give me the key, I'll open the door," Andrew said drawing back.

Ella drew in a deep breath and held out the key without a word. Andrew opened the lock and handed her the key again.

"Most probably, I'll be leaving tomorrow, Ella. I wish you all the best," Andrew put out a hand. "It was nice knowing you."

"All the best for your exhibition! It was nice knowing you," Ella shook his hand. She smiled brightly but something seemed to crack deep down in her heart.

"I must go then. I have things to do before I call it a night. Goodbye!" Andrew waved as he turned away.

"Goodbye..." Ella said softly as she watched him walk down the road instead of going to Mrs. Merryweather's home.

She shut the door and leaned against it, perplexed by a feeling she couldn't understand.

"Good morning, Ella!"

"Good morning, Hannah! What's going on? Why are there so many policemen around the castle?" Ella queried.

"The castle has been barricaded and so have the grounds. None of us can enter the grounds today," Hannah replied. "Haven't you seen the news?"

"What news? What's happened?" Ella asked confused.

"Some valuable artefacts have been stolen from the castle including the ancient Whitman dagger," Hannah spoke loudly trying to be heard over the din.

"What? When did this happen?"

"Last night, probably. That's what the news said," Hannah said.

"Did they find the culprits?" queried Ella, feeling sick suddenly.

"No, not yet. The police are trying to find clues. I think we better go to the cafe. We'll be needed there rather than here," Hannah suggested practically. "It doesn't look like these grounds will be opened today. What a shame!"

"Yes. Hannah, you go to the cafe. I'll come in a little later," Ella said thoughtfully.

"Where are you going?"

"I think I may know something... I need to meet Sheriff Jack," Ella said with passion.

"Ella... What? What is going on?" Hannah asked looking at her anxiously.

"Don't worry Hannah. I'll join you as soon as possible in the cafe. I need to go now before it's too late," Ella said hurrying off.

~

"You're absolutely sure about this, Ella?" asked Sheriff Jack walking down the quiet garden path.

"Quite sure, Sheriff," Ella nodded.

"Very well. Here we go then," Sherriff Jack rang the doorbell.

"Who's there?" called the voice from within.

Sheriff Jack nodded to Ella.

"It's me, Ella."

"Ella, just a minute. I'm coming!"

The latch clicked and the door swung open.

"Ella dear, what a lovely surprise! Why aren't you at the castle..." Mrs. Merryweather's voice trailed away when she saw the big, broad shouldered man standing on her doorstep in uniform. "And, who may this be?"

"Good morning, Mrs. Merryweather. This is Sheriff Jack," Ella said tensely. "And, this is Mrs. Merryweather, Sheriff."

"Nice to meet you, Madam. May we come in?" asked the sheriff tersely.

"Good morning, Sheriff. Please do come in. How may I help you?" Mrs. Merryweather asked leading the way in.

"I wonder if you've seen the news?" enquired the sheriff. He settled down on a sofa in the living room when Mrs. Merryweather indicated the seat.

Mrs. Merryweather looked at Ella and then at the sheriff sitting down herself. "No, I haven't. Should I have? I don't relish watching misery while I sip my early morning cup of tea or coffee."

"Mrs. Merryweather, the Whitman Castle is the scene of a great theft. Last night precious artefacts were stolen from the old part of the castle along with the famous Whitman dagger," Sheriff Jack filled her in with the details.

"O dear! How terrible!" gasped Mrs. Merryweather.

"Yes, it is a terrible thing to have happened," Sheriff Jack nodded.

"I hope the things are retrieved quickly and the culprits punished," Mrs. Merryweather said passionately.

"Well, we hope the same, Madam. But for this we will need your help," Sheriff Jack said.

"My help? I don't see how can I help you?" Mrs. Merryweather looked from the sheriff to Ella perplexed.

"Well, Mrs. Merryweather... You see, we have reason to believe that your paying guest could be involved in the theft. He has escaped after committing the crime..." Sheriff Jack said only to be interrupted.

"My paying guest? Do you mean, Andrew Anderson? How can you even think?" Mrs. Merryweather said incredulously.

"Mrs. Merryweather, remember last night he said he had to leave? He told me the same thing. And, today this has happened," Ella spoke up, trying to reason with the older woman.

"So what? It doesn't mean he robbed the castle, Ella. Does it?"

"But he said that his work is finished here and he has to go," Ella said.

"He's a photographer, Ella. He came here to click photographs," Mrs. Merryweather insisted. "That's not enough to suspect him."

"It may be a ruse for all we know. I can't forget the way he looked at the dagger that day when I took him around the old part of the castle... it... it... seemed strange," Ella said quietly. "Now I wish I hadn't taken him there."

"Look, Mrs. Merryweather. We need your help, we need you to think carefully and tell us if he mentioned anything or you saw anything which now makes you think was suspicious. It could be crucial in helping us nab him," Sheriff Jack said gently.

"To be honest, Sheriff... I never did see anything suspicious in the man. He's a wonderful young fellow with a heart of gold. I don't agree to this tommyrot about him robbing or anything," Mrs. Merryweather said hotly.

Ella walked to the older woman's sofa and knelt down beside her. She took her hands in hers and said earnestly, "Mrs. Merryweather, I know you thought highly of him but it turns out he was fooling us. See, if we don't act quickly he'll escape... out of reach and we'll never get all those heirlooms again. Please... please... help us. Have you any idea where he is?"

"Who are you talking about, Miss Wilson?" asked a familiar voice from the doorway.

Ella whipped around, stood up hurriedly and turned as pale as a sheet.

"Miss Wilson, are you alright? I hope you won't faint. You look as if you've seen a ghost. All good?" Andrew said advancing into the room. "I think you better sit down."

"I... I'm fine. Just that..." Ella stammered.

"Just that you hadn't expected to see me?" queried Andrew softly. His eyes danced mischievously.

"No... What are *you* doing here?" she asked finally. "You should have..."

"I should have?" queried Andrew with raised eyebrows.

"Are you Mr. Andrew Anderson?" enquired Sheriff Jack stepping in.

"Yes, Sheriff. I'm Andrew Anderson," Andrew said. "How can I help you?"

"Mr. Anderson, I request you to co-operate with me and accompany me to the police station for questioning," Sheriff Jack said in a businesslike voice.

"I'd love to co-operate with you, Sheriff. But for what is this questioning?" asked Andrew walking to a sofa and sitting down.

Jack looked at Ella and then at Andrew. "It's regarding the theft at Whitman Castle. You're a suspect and..."

"Wonderful! Do you have a warrant?" queried Andrew calmly.

"Well... No... But..." Sheriff Jack said hesitantly.

"Do you know, you can't do this? If I complain, you can face charges or worst lose your job," Andrew said silkily.

"Mr. Anderson, stop it. I brought the sheriff here. I told him that I suspect you," Ella said hotly. "I saw you... I saw the way you were looking at the dagger that day and you yourself told me last night that you had unfinished business you needed to attend to. You didn't come home but walked off down the road towards the castle."

"That proves nothing, Miss Wilson. Nothing at all! Looking at a dagger doesn't imply I intend robbing it nor does taking a walk after dinner. Stop being paranoid!" Andrew said sharply.

"Mr. Anderson, I suggest you be calm and lower your voice. Even if you claim you aren't the culprit you have been suspected. If you aren't at fault there's nothing to worry. This town is ours; the castle belongs to our town. Ella is merely trying to help and so am I. I request you to please co-operate with us," Sheriff Jack said quietly.

"Very well. I understand. I'll accompany you after I receive a phone call I'm expecting any moment now,"

Andrew said leaning further back in his sofa. He looked at the two people standing before him and smiled calmly.

'Tring- tring! Tring-tring!' The mobile phone rang precisely at that very moment.

"Hello? Yes? Is it? Wonderful! Well done! Yes, I'll just switch it on. Ok. Bye!" Andrew spoke mysteriously into his phone.

"Well? Shall we leave now?" Sheriff Jack said.

"Not before we've checked the news on the television," Andrew said walking to the table, picking up the remote and switching on the television. He flipped through a few channels before pausing at a local news channel.

The news reporter was saying...

"And, the Whitman dagger along with other precious things robbed last night has been retrieved. The gang known as the Clever Un's were responsible for carrying out the theft. They entered the castle last night and very cleverly tampered with the security cameras and other systems. Reports have come in from sources which say that the leader is a localite, Edward Evans. Some people have reported seeing him scouring the castle grounds a couple of days back..."

Ella gasped when a picture of him flashed on the screen.

Mrs. Merryweather exclaimed loudly, "This chap! He's their leader? Wasn't he the one who came to our stall that morning, Ella? Your childhood friend, he said he was. He took you around to meet all your friends, remember?"

"Yes! I thought... I didn't know..." Ella said in a shocked voice and sat down on the nearest chair.

"Miss Wilson, please drink some water. Mrs. Merryweather, I think we'll need some tea," Andrew said placing a glass in Ella's hand.

"Yes, Andrew dear. I'll get us all some hot strong tea," Mrs. Merryweather said hurrying into the kitchen.

"I'll be damned. This creep! Sleazy fellow! How dare he rob our town, our castle!" muttered Sheriff Jack under his breath.

"Don't worry, the Intelligence tracked him and knew what he was planning for quite a few days. He was wanted in other cases also. They waited to catch him red-handed with the loot so that he couldn't escape. I went out last night because the Intelligence updated me about the intended robbery," Andrew said quietly.

"Why the Intelligence updated you on it? Who are you?" enquired Sheriff Jack in awe.

"Now that, my good man, you will not believe if I tell you. So, let's wait a few minutes more. I'm expecting company," Andrew said with a smile, his eyes on Ella's shocked face.

"Let's all have a cup of tea," Mrs. Merryweather said pleasantly, carrying in the tray.

"Let me help you, Mrs. Merryweather," Andrew took the tray from her and placed it on the centre table. "Miss Wilson? Will you pour?"

Ella raised stormy eyes to his.

"I knew Andrew couldn't be wrong. I knew, I just knew," Mrs. Merryweather said sipping from her cup.

"Thank you, Mrs. Merryweather. At least you believed in me," Andrew looked at Ella with a boyish grin. "Miss Wilson was adamant to label me a thief."

"Mr. Anderson..." Ella began hotly only to be interrupted by the doorbell.

"That's for me. I'll open the door," Andrew kept his cup and saucer on the table and hurried to the door.

He re-entered with three men dressed in ordinary shirt and trousers. But they were huge like the sheriff and stern looking.

"Ladies, Sheriff, meet the Head of the Intelligence Team handling this affair here, Bob Burton. These are his assistants – George Dawson and Thomas Walker. This is the local Sheriff, Jack. And, of course you know these two wonderful ladies. Please sit down gentlemen." Andrew said introducing them.

"How do they know us?" Mrs. Merryweather asked surprised when they shook hands and were finally seated in the small living room that looked smaller now.

"Madam, because you were under our surveillance too. We couldn't let Lord Whitman stay just anywhere without providing him security. He was constantly being monitored and followed by his team of bodyguards," Thomas Walker said accepting the cup and saucer from Ella luckily before she dropped it.

"What?" Ella squeaked. "Lord Whitman?"

"By Jove!" Sheriff Jack exclaimed.

"You're Lord Whitman?" Mrs. Merryweather queried happily. "Oh dear God! I knew there was something special about you."

Andrew shrugged his shoulders gently. "Yes, I am. Guilty to the core of this and nothing else!"

"It's absolutely laughable to think you'd rob your own home," laughed Mrs. Merryweather aloud.

"What? Someone thought you robbed the Whitman Castle?" Bob Burton asked sharply.

"It was just a misunderstanding and nothing else, Bob. No need to worry about that," Andrew said laughing. He looked at Ella's face, which was flaming red. She bent to pour another cup of tea. "Everyone in this town believes the castle is a part of their home which is so heart warming. I'm glad I came here and met everyone."

"But why didn't you disclose your identity, Sir, Lord Whitman?" Sheriff Jack asked.

"First, I wanted a quiet holiday from all my work. I'm a business tycoon and it can get pretty stressful with the media following me around everywhere. So, when the Mayor contacted me with the proposal for a Spring Fair

I thought it was the perfect chance to slip away to a place where no one knew me. Second, it also gave me a good opportunity to meet the people without worrying they were being kind because I was the new Lord Whitman. Third, I could see the place, meet the people, and gauge the scope for investing more funds to upgrade this small, lovely town so that it can become a hub for more tourists," Andrew replied simply.

"Yes, and now it's out that the business tycoon Andrew Anderson Whitman, the new Lord Whitman is here, we cannot let you stay in this neighbourhood anymore. The media will be swarming all over the place in minutes. We request you to let us escort you to the castle, Sir. All arrangements have been made for your stay there," George Dawson said placing his cup and saucer on the table.

"Yes. I'll get my things from the room. Just give me a few minutes to say goodbye," Andrew said standing up.

"We'll be waiting outside for you," Bob nodded, standing up.

~

The days flew on wings. Easter Sunday dawned bright and clear.

"My dear people of God, let us thank the Almighty Father and His Son, our Redeemer for protecting us and our town from a tragedy. We also pray for the patron of our town, Lord Whitman and his family, may God bestow him with His choicest blessings. Let us close our eyes and pray for ourselves and our loved ones that our Risen Saviour will brighten our dark paths in the days to come..." the Pastor prayed during the morning service.

Ella, from where she sat beside Hannah and her family could see Andrew in his family's pew towering over the others. He looked handsome in his gray suit and tie. She hardly remembered what happened later that morning three days ago. Andrew had said a warm thank you to Mrs. Merryweather while hugging her, and she had got all emotional. As for herself, he had just nodded and shook hands. She hadn't said a word either. She felt so embarrassed.

At that moment the entire congregation began singing. She smiled at Mrs. Merryweather standing on her left who was singing loudly but quite out of tune. She silently thanked God that everything had worked out just fine. She glanced at her watch. The service was about to end, she gently touched Hannah's arm. Hannah nodded, they made their way out of the pew to the church's grounds. Jim and Joe were making the last minute arrangements to the breakfast laden tables. The delicious spread of sandwiches, cup cakes, fruit cake slices, hotdogs, chicken patties, wedges of fresh fruit, bagels, croissants, jugs of fresh fruit juice, tea and coffee waited for the church goers and other visitors. There were chocolate and vanilla flavoured Easter eggs for the children also. Hannah and Ella donned aprons over their dresses and waited.

“I was afraid that Andrew, I mean Lord Whitman will cancel the order,” Hannah said arranging the paper plates.

“Why would he cancel the breakfast?” asked Ella looking at her surprised.

“I don’t know. I felt he may take offense after that fiasco two-three days back. He’s a big man, Ella. They all have their whims and fancies,” Hannah said quickly, seeing the look on her face.

“Well, he didn’t and here we are. I think we should live in the present. Here come the people,” Ella said brightly.

“Good morning Pastor James. Happy Easter! What would you like to have with your coffee?” Hannah asked with a smile.

“Happy Easter! A sandwich and some fresh fruit would be just the thing. Isn’t it wonderful to have the new Lord Whitman with us? And, he’s such a generous man to have organized this breakfast for everyone,” the Pastor said happily. “God is great!”

“That’s so true. Here’s your plate,” Hannah said handing him a paper plate. “Have a great day!”

“Good morning Hannah! Happy Easter!” Andrew said walking up to her. He bent to kiss her on the cheek.

“Happy Easter Andrew... I mean Lord Whitman,” Hannah said courteously.

“No need to be so formal. I just told Mrs. Merryweather the same thing,” Andrew laughed. He looked at Mrs. Merryweather standing beside him, holding his arm.

"Here's a good fellow, like I always told you, Hannah dear. He'll always be Andrew to us. Won't you, dear?" Mrs. Merryweather said happily.

"Yes, I will. Now shall I get you something to have, Mrs. Merryweather? You must be famished," Andrew said kindly. "But first let me take you to those chairs there. See you, Hannah."

"See you, Andrew," Hannah said turning to a boy who wanted an Easter egg.

"Yes, I'm thirsty too. A cup of nice steaming tea would be great. And, a chicken patty with those dear little sandwiches are what I fancy," Mrs. Merryweather said sitting down on a chair. "Did you meet Ella and speak to her?"

"I tried but she's been avoiding me like the plague," laughed Andrew. "I'll try once again."

"Yes dear. She must be upset about mistaking you as she did," Mrs. Merryweather said kindly.

"I'll get you some breakfast," Andrew said walking to the table where Ella was helping the guests serve themselves.

"Hello Miss Wilson. Happy Easter!" Andrew said.

"Hello. Happy Easter, Lord Whitman. How can I help you?"

"I'm looking for some sandwiches and a chicken patty for a friend of mine sitting there. Do you think you can help me?" Andrew said pointing to Mrs. Merryweather sitting on a chair not far away, who in turn waved and smiled at Ella.

"Sure, do you need anything else?" Ella said smiling at Mrs. Merryweather and loading a plate with the required food items.

"Yes, I want to speak to you for a few minutes," Andrew said.

"At the moment that's not possible. I'm busy as you can see," Ella said with a smile.

"Of course. I just need a moment. There's nothing much I want to say except thank you for everything you've done for me and the Whitman Castle. I'll be leaving tomorrow. I wish you all the best for the future," Andrew said. "See you later in the castle grounds for the rally and the prize giving. I hope you'll think of me as a friend. You carry on with your work. I won't disturb you anymore."

Ella stared at him open-mouthed as he picked up the tray with the plates and coffee cups.

"Goodbye, Miss Wilson. Take care."

"It's been five months. September is coming to an end. She goes to her cafe and comes back. She hardly says a word about him but..."

"But what Lucia?" Gabriella asked looking up from the game of scrabble they were playing. "I've made my word. Come, it's your turn now. Stop looking out of the window."

Mrs. Lucia Merryweather let the curtains drop and resumed her seat at the living room table again. "I don't know what to do. I've never felt so helpless. I know she loves him. I can feel it. S-I-L-E-N-T... There that's my word. She's gone all quiet."

"Hmm... Y-E-A-R-N. She's missing him, Lucia. Her soul is yearning for him," Gabriella said. "Your turn."

"But the silly girl won't admit it. She'll smile and act all cheerful in front of everyone. S-P-A-R-K-L-E. The sparkle is missing from her eyes and voice. I'm afraid I'll lose her again. I don't know what to do."

Gabriella gazed at the board carefully before placing her letters on the board. "E-M-B-E-R-S. My dear Lucia, the embers of her love are still ablaze deep down. Just a spark is required! What if Andrew comes here again? Can you make that happen?"

"Whoopiiee!" Lucia exclaimed joyfully. "I knew it. A good game of scrabble and a conversation with you can solve any problem. I'll start working on that."

"You're welcome, Lucia. But be careful you don't break any Fairyland rules. You cannot force them to come together. Are you sure Andrew loves her?" Gabriella looked at her in concern.

"Yes. Of course he does. Don't forget he was living with me in this very house. I could feel his heart beating whenever he looked at her. I truly wish he had kissed her just once..." Lucia said solemnly. "And, my word is... K-I-S-S."

"The kiss of true love isn't so easily achieved, Lucia. You know it. And, for Ella it has to happen at the castle. Have you forgotten? It's written in the stars. D-E-S-T-I-N-Y. It's destined that the one she kisses in the castle will be her forever love."

"Yes, yes. The stars have started revealing their mysteries for Ella. She's to find her true love in the castle," Mrs. Merryweather said.

"Exactly, so you need to be sure it's Andrew and not someone else," Gabriella said looking at her.

"It is Andrew, Gabriella. I know it. I just know it," Lucia Merryweather said earnestly. "They are P-E-R-F-E-T-T-O together."

"Lucia, why do you do this?" Gabriella looked at her in exasperation.

"What did I do?" asked Lucia innocently.

"Why do you keep making words in other languages while playing scrabble in English?"

"Did I?"

"Yes. Perfetto is an Italian word," Gabriella said looking at Lucia crossly.

"Oh dear! But Ella and Andrew are perfect together, they're perfect for each other," Lucia said smiling. "Aren't they Gabriella? Say 'yes'. Come now, don't sulk over a word. Go beyond mere words."

"Very well, dear Lucia. They're perfetto. You've got to get cracking. Reach out to Andrew, and see what happens," Gabriella said. "And, by the way I just remembered your wish for Ella."

"My wish? Which one?"

"*My dear godchild Ella, may your heart be touched by love soon. And, when it does... the snow will melt, flowers will blossom and fill the air with a sweet fragrance. Birds and bees will sing songs of love and togetherness, and rabbits with hares will dance and make merry. I wish with my whole heart that you find your true love, your soul mate.*" Gabriella repeated the words Lucia had enunciated months ago. "This one. Remember?"

"Yes, o yes! How could I have forgotten? It was spring when they met, flowers were blossoming, birds and bees were singing songs of love. Gabriella, thank you for reminding me," Lucia said happily. "Theirs is a love that's meant to be. I only have to give another little push. They need to meet once again."

"Yes, Lucia. And, after all 'absence does make the heart grow fonder', doesn't it? You yourself have said that Ella is pining for her young man," Gabriella said happily.

"And, I'm hopeful that Andrew hasn't forgotten Ella. He must be thinking of her, dreaming of her," Lucia said and clasped her hands.

"And, there's only one way to find out. Talk to him," Gabriella said.

"Yes, talk to him," Lucia said.

"Go on, talk to him then," Gabriella urged Lucia. "Lucia, don't tell me! Do you have any way of getting in touch with the man, or not?"

"Gabriella, am I Ella's fairy godmother or not?" Lucia said. "Humans use mobile phones to speak with each other. I have the numerical code that's required to speak to Andrew."

"Wonderful! Then... speak to him. I'm excited to see this love story unfurl," Gabriella said eagerly.

"Right away... and... here goes the call..." Lucia clicked on the number in her mobile phone.

~

"Ella? What are you thinking about?" Hannah asked after she noticed Ella for the third time that afternoon looking lost.

"Nothing. Nothing at all, Hannah. I think I'm a bit tired," Ella said smiling.

"By any chance are you thinking of Andrew? There was an article in the newspaper with photographs from the grand exhibition he had mentioned," Hannah said placing a cup of coffee before her.

"No. I'm not thinking of him," Ella said quietly.

"There was a picture of you laughing and talking to children at the Spring Fair. You looked so happy then," Hannah said softly.

Ella closed her eyes and sighed. She turned to Hannah with a smile. "I'm happy now, Hannah. See... I'm smiling."

"Yes, you're smiling. But that isn't the same, is it, Ella? You can talk to me," Hannah said holding her hand.

"I know Hannah, I can talk to you. But there isn't anything to talk about. I'm fine," Ella said brightly. "Thank you for the coffee, Hannah."

"You're welcome, Ella."

"Hannah," Ella said as Hannah turned away. "Would you mind if I left you to look after the cafe? It's early October and I want to go and take a walk in the castle's Rose Garden before this year's roses fade away."

"No problem at all, Ella. I'll be here with the others. You go and take a look at those roses. I know how much you loved going there with your father and mother. Your dear mother used to get armfuls of the blooms for the cafe. The gardeners were so generous," Hannah said reminiscing.

"Lord Whitman was a very kind man. He used to tell the gardeners to indulge mother with the flowers she loved so much," Ella smiled nostalgically.

"The new Lord Whitman is no less kind. He's kept his promise to help boost the trade in our town. I heard he's planning a Halloween Festival to lure more tourists at the end of the month," Hannah supplied folding a hand towel.

"That's good. We better find out more about the plans so that we too can prepare," Ella said. "I better go or it will start getting dark before I get a chance to drink in the beauty of the roses to my heart's content."

"See you tomorrow, Ella. Bye!"

"See you, Hannah!"

Ella walked through the castle grounds. The castle's window panes gleamed in the light of the evening sun. It was quiet all around except for the occasional sound of a thrush singing somewhere. The huge trees were preparing themselves for a brilliant display of their best colours. Spring and Summer had given way to early Autumn. She looked at the slowly yellowing leaves and inhaled the fresh air. She took a left and opened a quaint white gate quite hidden from the view of strangers.

She stopped and looked in delight at the roses blooming in profusion. Red, pink, white, peach, yellow... there were bushes, and creepers spilling over with the last of the year's blossoms. Butterflies flitted from flower to flower happily unaware of the coming winter. Bees hastened around collecting the nectar they needed before the pretty blooms disappeared. Ella walked down the path in the private garden of the Whitman Castle lost in the beauty and heady fragrance, reliving memories of her childhood days. She suddenly looked up and saw the balcony that she had showed Andrew that afternoon from the ballroom. That afternoon... she thought, seemed ages ago. She sighed and sat down on a marble bench.

The music from the fountains soothed her. The clouds in the sky floated in different patterns. She thought she spied a knight riding a horse which steadily changed into two hearts intertwined with each other. The sun was beginning to sink over the horizon and the birds were calling out to each other as they flew to their nests. They flocked in large numbers making a regular din, shattering the silence. The clouds first blushed pink, then turned orange as they reflected the dying daylight. Ella sat there oblivious to everything except the beauty of Nature around her and therefore, was startled when she heard her name.

"Ella..."

"Mr. Anderson, I mean Lord Whitman. Good evening. I didn't know you were here," Ella said breathlessly, she stood up abruptly.

Andrew took in the confusion in her eyes and the heightened colour of her cheeks. He felt a stirring in his heart and wondered for the thousandth time why did he stay away so long from her.

"Good evening, Miss Wilson. I just arrived a little while ago. I'm sorry, I didn't mean to disturb you," Andrew said quietly, looking at her face, drinking in her beauty.

"You need not apologize. You've not disturbed me. I was on the point of leaving anyway."

"Please stay, don't leave on my account. I just happened to come this way," Andrew said.

"It will be getting dark soon," Ella said. "I should go."

"Would you like to have a cup of tea? Some refreshments?" Andrew offered, trying to stall her.

"No. Thank you so much. But, I really should be going," Ella said hurriedly.

"In that case, I'll ask someone to drive you home." Andrew suggested.

"Lord Whitman, you're very generous. I couldn't dream of troubling you," Ella said taken aback.

"Very well, then, let me walk you back? I've been travelling the entire day and I'm much in need of some exercise. It will do me a world of good," Andrew insisted and added, "What's more I can meet Mrs. Merryweather for a couple of minutes!"

Ella drew in a deep breath and said, "Alright then..."

"After you..." Andrew said stepping to the side.

He followed her through the castle grounds keeping up a steady conversation, enquiring about everyone in the town, avoiding any direct reference to either him or her.

Ella answered appropriately, she glanced at him from beneath her eyelashes a couple of times as they walked through the roads in the gathering dusk and finally reached her home. He quietly took the key from her and opened the door for her before handing the key back. He waited for her to go in, bid her a goodbye and then turned to walk away when she shut the door.

~

"Andrew! My dear, dear Andrew!" said Mrs. Merryweather jubilantly hugging him when she opened the door and saw who rang her doorbell. "I'm so happy to see you."

"Good evening, Mrs. Merryweather. I'm glad to see you. Had I known I would receive such a marvellous welcome I would have come earlier," Andrew said smoothening down his hair as he stepped into the living room.

"Never you mind, my boy. Each time you come here you'll receive an equally glowing welcome. And, don't expect me to call you Lord Whitman or keep up all those curtsies and all. For me, you are Andrew, just Andrew, the young man who stayed with me for a couple of days at the time of the Spring Fair," Mrs. Merryweather said and laughed merrily.

"And, I wouldn't expect you to follow any of that traditional stuff, Mrs. Merryweather. That's for others not for you," Andrew conceded.

"What about your bodyguards? Where are they?" Mrs. Merryweather asked suddenly realizing he was a big shot, and expecting someone to bang on the door or jump down the chimney.

"Oh... I didn't tell them where I was going. I sort of slipped away. Actually, I saw Ella in the Rose Garden in the castle and I walked her home," Andrew said hastily, trying to avoid her sharp gaze.

"You walked Ella home. Ok... alright. That's why you're here," Mrs. Merryweather nodded with satisfaction.

She pouted and continued, "And, here was I thinking you came to see me."

"Mrs. Merryweather please stop pulling my legs. You know you told me that night I should be a gentleman and walk Ella home, even if it was across the road, then how could I let her come all the way alone from the castle, that too when it was beginning to get dark?" Andrew tried to sound practical.

"That's perfectly alright. I can understand," Mrs. Merryweather smiled knowingly.

"Really?" laughed Andrew. "What?"

Mrs. Merryweather looked at him calmly, smiled and said, "Your heart beats for her, Andrew. Doesn't it?"

Andrew gazed at the old woman standing in front of him, so serene, so motherly. "Yes. Yes," he whispered. "I love her, I love Ella. I can't take this anymore. I can't hide what I feel anymore, Mrs. Merryweather."

"Andrew... I can't say how happy I am," Mrs. Merryweather said happily, tears streaming down her face. "You're perfect for each other."

Andrew laughed. "Wow! That's a pleasant surprise. At least someone thinks we're perfect together."

"Why do you say that, boy?" chided Mrs. Merryweather.

"Because Ella doesn't! She... Well, I don't know what she feels. Sometimes I feel she does have feelings for me, the next minute I'm not so sure. Sometimes I feel she enjoys my company and then the very next minute I feel she can't wait to get away from me. These five months have been hell for me. I couldn't get her out of my mind. My dreams, my waking moments... she's been there every minute, every second," Andrew said running his hands anxiously through his hair. "I don't know what to do. I can't live without her. I kept away thinking that it was some infatuation, it would fade away but the feeling has only grown with time."

Mrs. Lucia Merryweather watched him with growing hope and excitement.

"Now, now! Andrew, please sit down. I guess this needs some careful consideration and planning. Let me get us both some tea and then we'll discuss the matter in detail," Mrs. Merryweather said eagerly. "You better call up to your head of security and tell them where you are because this will take some time and they'll panic if they don't find you in the castle. Do stay for dinner."

"You think we can work this out?" Andrew asked her in disbelief.

"Why not? You love her. And, love coupled with hope is enough to win the world. You've just got to win your lady love's heart. How difficult can that be? When will you use all that charm you have?" Mrs. Merryweather said mischievously.

"So Andrew, you mentioned that you're planning a Halloween Festival at the end of this month?" Mrs. Merryweather said eating dessert.

"Yes, it will bring in more tourists and it will be a good opportunity for the local crowd to earn more," Andrew said relishing the custard with jelly.

"Andrew! Seriously! Will you stop thinking about the town?" Mrs. Merryweather said pausing with the spoon halfway to her mouth.

"I'm sorry, Mrs. Merryweather. Did I say something wrong?"

"No, my dear boy. But you've got to think how you can you use this opportunity to get closer to Ella," Mrs. Merryweather said thinking.

"Ok... How can I do that? Promote her cafe? Spend time in her cafe?" Andrew said considering options.

"Andrew, you've got to think of something more romantic. You young men these days have no idea of romancing your girls," Mrs. Merryweather grumbled. "Think of something big, something that will give you a chance of getting close to her, holding her close, kissing her..."

"Ahem... Mrs. Merryweather. I don't think that's going to be easy," Andrew said doubtfully.

"Rubbish! It's not that difficult either. I know what... you can dance with her. If you dance with her, you get to hold her close to you and even kiss her," Mrs. Merryweather said excitedly.

"Wait a minute! I'm lagging behind... How will I dance with her?" Andrew looked at her confused.

"I'll tell you! I have it all pictured in my mind... You're to have a Ball in the castle to culminate the Halloween Festival, a fancy dress. You know the one where everyone dresses up like someone... wizards, witches, frogs, actors, actresses, princesses, and princes, whatever. There will be food, wine, singing, dancing, and you'll dance the evening away with the woman you love. You'll hold her close to you, where she can feel your heart beating for her; she can gaze into your eyes and see the love shining there..." Mrs. Merryweather spoke excitedly and paused for a breath.

Andrew looked at her in amazement and then leaned across the table to hug her.

"What a brilliant idea, Mrs. Merryweather! I love you."

"Ahh... My boy! No fibbing. You love Ella!" laughed the old lady. "But I'll forgive you because I understand what you mean."

"So, when shall I begin working on this plan?" Andrew queried, sitting down once again.

"From tomorrow itself! But you're to woo your woman slowly and gracefully as we discussed. Take one day at a time. Ella isn't like all those city girls, she's different. She's been hurt before, so she's terrified of letting anyone close to her again. She's more like a terrified gazelle who's been abused, you'll need to pursue her gently," Mrs. Merryweather said kindly.

"Yes, I'll keep that in mind. I can't afford to lose her," Andrew nodded with understanding.

"Andrew, are you sure this is what you want?" Mrs. Merryweather asked solemnly. "Quite sure?"

"Mrs. Merryweather, I understand your concern. Yes, I'm sure. Absolutely sure, I want Ella in my life for forever, as my wife. I'm willing to do anything, even wait for eternity to be with her," Andrew said, his eyes blazing with determination.

"Amen!" whispered Mrs. Merryweather with tears shining in her eyes.

~

"Good morning, Hannah. How are you?" Andrew said walking into the cafe.

"Good morning, Lord Whitman. I'm good. How are you?" Hannah replied.

"Hannah, not you also. This was one reason I didn't want to reveal my true identity. It creates a distance," Andrew said sitting down at a table near one of the windows. "Could I have your special coffee? No one can make it the way you do. And, please call me Andrew."

"Yes, Lord... I mean Andrew. I'll get your coffee," Hannah said brightly, hurrying away.

Andrew looked about him. He loved this place. It had all the warmth anyone was looking for. It wasn't just a cafe. It was more than that. He wondered if it was because of the courtesy of the staff or the magic of the woman he loved. He smiled as he thought of her and how he was going to try to win her love.

"Here's your coffee, Andrew. Just like you like it," Hannah said placing a cup and almond cookies on the table.

"Thank you, Hannah. Won't you join me for a little chat?" Andrew invited her, drawing out a chair.

"A little chat?" Hannah looked surprised.

"Yes, it's been a long time we met. And, there aren't many customers," Andrew said looking about them. "It's early in the morning. And, Ella isn't here either."

"Alright. Though if Ella was here she wouldn't mind. She's been missing you herself even if she doesn't say..." Hannah quickly put a hand over her mouth. "I don't think I should have said that."

Andrew's eyes gleamed. He digested this unexpected piece of information and stored it away for further contemplation. "I didn't hear anything. So how have you been? How's the business going?"

"The cafe is doing extremely well. We've had a regular stream of tourists pouring in the town after the Spring Fair. We, of course are grateful to you for all the efforts you've put in," Hannah said gratefully.

"That's of no consequence. I guess that robbery added to the buzz, with the media swooping down on the scene and creating a regular to-do," Andrew said sipping the coffee. "Ahh… this is absolutely divine. Do you think Ella will let you go if I want to take you with me?"

"For this coffee? Then it would be better that you take Ella with you. I learnt to make this coffee from her?" Hannah laughed.

"Will she come with me?" Andrew asked looking straight at her. "Will she leave all this and come with me, halfway across the globe?"

"Andrew, love is a funny thing. When one loves… they cross oceans, climb mountains to be with the one they love. The day Ella falls in love she'll do the same," Hannah said quietly.

Andrew sighed and then said brightly. "You're right. Anyway, I'll be meeting the Mayor today to discuss the Halloween Festival I have in mind, and a Costume Ball on the last day. So, there'll be more tourists pouring in during the last week of October. I want to work out the advertisement and marketing strategies and get them into place. I'll be keeping a close watch on all the proceedings. So, I'll be here for the next few weeks. I'll keep meeting you and demanding this awesome coffee."

"Andrew, why have you come here?" Hannah asked softly.

"To drink this wonderful coffee and catch up with you, Hannah," Andrew laughed, taking another sip.

"I mean... Why have you come to our town again? You're a man of great resources. You could have planned and executed the entire Halloween Festival sitting in one of your posh offices; you could have sent someone else to take care of everything. I'm sure you have hundreds of willing and competent employees," Hannah said looking at him carefully, sipping his coffee.

"What do you think, Hannah?" Andrew said looking at her over the rim of his cup.

"Is it because of Ella?" Hannah asked hopefully.

"Why else, Hannah?" Andrew queried with a slow smile and a shrug.

"Sweet Lord in Heaven! Is this true? Am I truly hearing what you're saying?" Hannah squeaked, tears shining in her eyes.

"Yes, Hannah. You heard me right!" Andrew smiled. "And, is it true what you said that she has been missing me?"

"Yes, that's what I think. She's been all quiet and thoughtful after you left," Hannah said. "I can't think of any other reason."

"It could be that she feels uncomfortable for mistakenly thinking that I robbed the castle?" Andrew suggested.

"Maybe... But there's something else deep down... Something she doesn't want to accept. I know she's terrified of losing control, of placing her trust in someone else. She's been hurt, Andrew. You don't know how painful it is to have your trust shattered," Hannah said earnestly.

"I can understand, Hannah. And, I can assure you I won't hurt her. I don't want to see her in pain ever," Andrew said squeezing Hannah's hand on the table. "Not if I can help it."

"If that's true, I pray that God will bring your heart's desire to fruition. Oh... I'm so happy. Manifestations are true. Do you know what I had told Ella when we came to know that the new Lord Whitman had agreed to open the castle grounds for the Spring Fair?" Hannah asked excitedly.

"Don't tell me!" Andrew said and laughed aloud.

"Yes, Ella was not willing to even think about it," Hannah laughed.

"No wonder she was so adamant to think that the new Lord Whitman was an old man... an invalid," Andrew guffawed, suddenly realizing that the Universe had meant them to meet.

He was going to make sure that Ella fell in love with him, however long it took. He would win her over. He needed to be calm and patient.

"Good morning, Ella."

"Good morning, Hannah. How's everything? Sorry, I got a bit late. Shall we start working on that new batch of chocolate chip cookies?" Ella said hanging her coat.

"Yes, absolutely. Also, we need to start planning about that Halloween Festival and the menu we will be serving during the week," Hannah said eagerly.

"But, is it certain we're having the festival?" Ella asked chewing her lip thoughtfully.

"Of course, why else do you think Andrew is in town?" Hannah reasoned.

"You know Andrew is in town?"

"Yes, I do. Do you know he's in town?" Hannah asked surprised. "You didn't tell me."

"There's nothing to tell. I just happened to meet him last evening in the Rose Garden of the castle and he walked me home," Ella said tying her apron.

"Ohhh..." Hannah said, sounding thoughtful.

"Hannah? What's that for?"

"Nothing. Did you offer him tea or a meal? It must've been getting supper time," Hannah queried again, measuring the ingredients.

"No, he just left me at the door and went."

"He went away just like that?" Hannah asked innocently.

"He went to Mrs. Merryweather's place."

"Ok. Mrs. Merryweather must've definitely offered him a meal. She's a real sweetheart," Hannah said.

"Hmm… He was there until quite late."

"How do you know, Ella?" Hannah asked.

"A car was outside with his bodyguard waiting for him," Ella supplied.

"So, you were waiting and watching for Andrew?" Hannah remarked, stirring the batter.

"Hannah! Why would I wait and watch for him?" Ella questioned her with faint impatience.

"How would I know Ella? You've made it clear hundreds of times that you feel nothing for him. So, if you know how long he was at Mrs. Merryweather's place, it's definitely not because you have feelings for him," Hannah said innocently.

"Hannah, what's come over you this morning?" Ella asked exasperatedly.

"Nothing Ella, nothing! Let's get the first batch of these cookies into the oven," Hannah said carrying the tray to the furnace with a smile. "By the way, you need to meet Sam. He was asking for you."

~

"Good evening, Sam," called Ella cheerfully, as she entered his small shop later that evening.

"A very good evening, Miss Ella. How's life?"

"All good. You wanted to see me?" Ella enquired.

"Yes, yes. My hens have laid the best of eggs. So, I thought I should tell you to purchase your stock as soon as possible. Also, Lord Whitman intends to offer a higher price for the eggs and chicken towards the end of the month. Don't you think that's wonderful? He's planning to have the biggest dance party at the castle. There will be food and drinks all night. A team of chefs is coming from his part of the world," Sam said happily.

"That's great news. Thank you for thinking of me. It's early October... I think four or five dozen eggs would suffice for the cakes and other goodies we make, to last till the end of October. Will you send it over to the cafe tomorrow morning? I'll make the payments at the discounted rate, on delivery," Ella said.

"Alright. I'll have your order delivered by afternoon. You tell Hannah and Jim to be ready," Sam said with a broad smile. Now that's done. What would you like me to give you just now?" Sam asked eagerly.

Ella smiled, "I would like a chicken. Don't cut it into pieces. I plan to make a roast. Then... half a dozen eggs and half a pound of that fresh yellow butter."

"Certainly!" grinned Sam. "Give me a few minutes."

"Good evening, Sam."

Ella's heart began to beat wildly at the sound of the voice she recognized so well.

"Good evening, my Lord. How can I help you?"

"I just came to confirm the order for 31st October. My staff will get in touch with you and collect the order as they feel appropriate a day or two before or as they deem necessary. This is the advance payment," Andrew held out an envelope to the man who beamed with excitement.

"You heard that, Miss Ella? What did I just tell you?" Sam said happily.

Ella nodded and then turned to Andrew.

"Hello Lord Whitman. Nice to meet you," Ella said courteously.

"Hello Miss Wilson! What coincidence! Nice to meet you again," Andrew said with extreme politeness.

Ella looked him suspiciously.

"So, how come you're here, Miss Wilson?" Andrew asked.

"I came to place a few orders for my cafe," Ella said quietly.

"Very good. Sam's the best, and his poultry items are excellent," Andrew said smiling at the busy man.

"Thank you, Lord Whitman. Thank you!" Sam beamed as he packed Ella's purchases. "Here you go Miss Ella. This packet has the chicken and this has the six eggs and butter."

"Thank you, Sam. How much?" Ella enquired before paying him. "I'll see you tomorrow."

"Goodbye. Do come again, Miss Ella," he said happily.

"Shall I help you, Miss Wilson?" Andrew said taking the packets from her.

"I'll manage. I've not very far to go. You needn't worry, Lord Whitman."

"I insist, Miss Wilson. I can't allow you to walk home alone, carrying packets, while I just stand by and watch. However mean you may think me to be, I do have royal blood in my veins and a good upbringing my mother insisted I have," Andrew said looking at her with determination.

Ella inhaled sharply. "But I don't think you're mean. Why would you say that?"

"I don't know, I somehow feel that you don't have a very good opinion of me. You think I'm a callous creature," Andrew said falling into step beside her.

"Lord Whitman, please stop embarrassing me. I beg you," Ella said turning to look at him. "I think nothing of the sort. Please, put your mind to rest."

"If that's the truth, then I think I can breathe a bit more freely," Andrew said with a satisfied smile.

After a short silence Ella queried, "Sam said that you're organizing a dance party? Is it for your friends from the business world?"

Andrew laughed. "Not just a dance party, it's a Halloween Costume Ball. I thought we can culminate the Halloween Festival with dance and food and music, a sort of celebration. I've spoken to the Mayor. It'll be at the castle."

"How wonderful! In the ballroom? It's been a while since there was a celebration at the castle," Ella said.

"Yes, in the ballroom. It will be a grand affair," Andrew said. "You of course, will come too. Won't you?"

"We've reached. Thank you, Lord Whitman for helping me," Ella said hurriedly. "I'll take those packets."

"The key?" Andrew stretched out his hand for the key.

"Ohh..." Ella said handing him the key.

"Ella, you just mentioned a while ago that you don't think of me as a mean fellow. Right?" Andrew said opening the lock of her house.

"Yes..." Ella said quietly, wondering where this was going.

"So, if I request you to join me for tea at the castle tomorrow at 4:00 p.m. I hope you'll honour me with your company," Andrew said pushing the door open and waiting on the doorstep.

"Well... Well..." Ella hesitated.

"You don't have to say 'yes' if you don't want to. I'll understand," Andrew said quickly. "I was just hoping you'll tell me a little more about the castle, as you seem to know more about it than I do. And, it's lovely to know about the place where I'm living currently."

"I can't see any reason to say 'I won't come'," Ella said a little breathlessly. "Yes... Yes. I'll be there. Thank you."

"Thank you, Miss Wilson. Shall I pick you up at 3:30 p.m. from your cafe?" Andrew asked quietly.

"Ok."

"See you tomorrow, Miss Wilson. Goodnight."

Ella smiled and nodded. "Goodnight."

"Good evening Miss Ella. It's wonderful to have you here," said the old butler pouring tea.

"Good evening, Mathew. Thank you," Ella smiled.

"Mathew, you too know Ella. That's great," Andrew said.

"Yes sir, I had often carried a tray to the library where her father sat reading those huge books on the castle and its history. Miss Ella would accompany her father at times," Mathew said with a wry smile. "The late Lord Whitman would spend a lot of time discussing the old days with Mr. Wilson."

"That's the reason why I've invited Ella over, to share memories of those days with me. I want to know about the rich past of my home and my people," Andrew said with a smile.

"We're happy, my Lord that you are taking such a keen interest in the castle and the town," the old butler said in his dry as dust voice, even if his eyes shone with joy.

"Does that mean that everyone thought since I'm not born and brought up here I'll not be interested?" laughed Andrew.

"People are free to think, Sir. It doesn't and can't affect who or what we are until we want it to," Mathew said wisely.

"Very true, Mathew. Now, how about serving us a slice of that delicious cake your wife bakes? I know Miss Wilson cooks marvellously well but even she can't beat this one," Andrew said good-naturedly.

"I know which cake you're speaking of Lord Whitman. Clara is a genius. I remember trailing along with my father as a child. And, to be honest, at times it would just be for a slice of that heavenly cake," Ella said smiling.

"Clara will be thrilled that you remember, Miss Ella. Here's a slice for you," Mathew placed a plate in front of her on the ancient dining table.

"Mathew, could we meet Clara after tea?" Andrew asked as the butler served him the cake. "I know how busy you all are running everything smoothly here, but just for a couple of minutes."

"Yes, my Lord. I'm sure she'd love to come up here," Mathew said with a bland face. But his voice betrayed the joy. "Would you like anything else?"

"No, nothing else. We'll help ourselves," Andrew said in a friendly manner.

Mathew withdrew with a bow and shut the huge doors behind him.

"So, Miss Wilson... Tell me something about this marvellous dining room. It's beautiful, no doubt but I know nothing of it except that once when I came here as a boy of eight, I used it to conceal myself. My cousins and I were playing hide and seek," Andrew said eating the cake.

"You came here as a boy?" Ella's eyes flew to his face.

"Yes, just once. And, I hid there... behind a damask curtain for more than an hour," Andrew laughed pointing to a spot.

"Really?" Ella asked looking at him with disbelief trying to imagine him as a boy.

"Well, yes. And, by the time I came out supper was over and I would have had to go to bed hungry had it not been for Clara smuggling some bread and butter for me," Andrew said confidentially. "Don't tell anyone, I told you that. I can't afford to let people know. It doesn't go with the image."

Ella laughed.

Andrew looked at her and smiled. She looked lovely. There was hope... he thought.

~

"Good morning, Ella dear."

"Good morning, Mrs. Merryweather," chirped Ella into the phone.

"How are you, my dear? Had breakfast?"

"I've never been better. And no, I've not had breakfast yet. I'm wondering what to eat," laughed Ella.

"Then why not join me for breakfast? I've made pancakes," Mrs. Merryweather invited her.

"Pancakes? Wow! But really there's no need to trouble yourself..." Ella began only to be silenced.

"Really Ella! By now you should know me better than that. You get here this minute, young lady. I'm waiting for you," Mrs. Merryweather said sternly.

"Alright… I'll be there in five minutes," Ella laughed.

~

"Hmm… these are delicious. Mrs. Merryweather you are awesome," Ella said eating another mouthful. "What's better than yummy pancakes on an autumn morning!"

"I'm glad you like them, dear. Have more!"

"No… No. Though I'm tempted, I mustn't. I've been eating too much lately," Ella said ruefully.

"You don't eat enough is what I feel. A young girl like you should be well rounded but you're way too lean," Mrs. Merryweather said eyeing her.

"Mrs. Merryweather, I'm putting on weight," Ella laughed. "Clara prepares such lovely food that I can't help but eat all the dishes she sends in."

"Clara?" queried Mrs. Merryweather. "Who's Clara? I've never heard you speaking of her before."

"Clara and Mathew work at the Castle. In fact, they've been there for years. My father and I would often meet them when we went there. Clara is a master chef. She can turn even the plainest ingredients into a master dish," Ella said drizzling some honey on a bite sized piece of pancake.

"Oh… so how come you're sampling her food these days?" Mrs. Merryweather asked curiously trying not to laugh.

"Well, Andr... I mean Lord Whitman asked me over a couple of times to tell him about the castle and the town. He's working on bringing out the historical aspect of our town to attract more people who love local art, food, customs and traditions," Ella said placing the fork on her empty plate.

"Wonderful! How's the Halloween Festival going? I can see a lot of activity on the streets the entire day," Mrs. Merryweather asked.

"Yes, it's very busy these days. Even at the cafe we hardly get any time to take a short break. Our ovens are working overtime too. Jim and Joe and Hannah are doing a splendid job," Ella said with a broad smile. "There are two days more to go for 31st October. I'm really exhausted, I was thinking of eating an apple for breakfast. Thank you for these heavenly pancakes. I'll be able to go without food at least till tea-time."

"It's nothing, dear. And, there's no need to go without lunch. I'll be preparing sandwiches for you and the others in the cafe," Mrs. Merryweather said kindly.

"Mrs. Merryweather, there's no need..."

"Did I ask you if there's a need or not? I'll be there around 12:30 p.m. While you gobble the sandwiches, I'll try my hand at attending to your customers. I know I won't be as good as you all, but still I can help a bit," Mrs. Merryweather said in her best bossy voice.

"Ok, madam. We'll look forward to seeing you with your special sandwiches," Ella said happily.

"Ella, I've heard there's a Costume Ball on 31st, isn't it? What are you wearing?" Mrs. Merryweather asked innocently.

"Well... I'm not sure I'll be going, Mrs. Merryweather," Ella said carrying her plate to the sink and washing it.

"Why ever not dear?" Mrs. Merryweather asked alarmed.

"I'm planning to spend a quiet evening at home. Everyone's invited to the castle, the town folk as well as the visitors. There's no need to keep the cafe open and I can rest after the mad rush of the entire week," Ella said wiping her hands on a hand towel.

"Come on, you're a young girl. You keep working all the time. You take no holidays. You need to have some fun," Mrs. Merryweather insisted.

"Well, resting at home is my idea of having fun. I'll wash my hair, do my nails and watch some television in the peace and quiet of my home," Ella laughed.

"How boring! You sound like an old lady!" Mrs. Merryweather snorted. "Shouldn't you be there in the castle dancing and having a gala time after working hard the entire week? You deserve the change."

"Mrs. Merryweather, I know you mean well but I'm not interested," Ella said hugging her.

"Is that the only reason? Or are you trying to avoid Andrew? Are you still annoyed with him?" Mrs. Merryweather queried point blank.

"No... I'm not annoyed with him. He's... He's a good person. He's doing so much for everyone here. I mean, he's left all his work to stay here and monitor everything personally. Isn't that great?" Ella said.

"I'm glad you don't dislike him like earlier. Then why aren't you willing to go for the Ball, Ella?" Mrs. Merryweather exclaimed.

"I never disliked him. It's... It's... only... I don't know what I felt for him. And, I still don't know what I feel about him," Ella sighed. "Alright, what am I going to wear to the Ball? I don't have any costume and I guess everything's been picked by now. So... it's simple. I can't go for the Ball."

23

"I'm coming... I'm coming! Stop banging on the door, for heaven's sake!" Ella shouted. Someone had been knocking on her door incessantly while she was soaking in her bathtub.

"Who is it?" she called reaching the door in her dressing gown, her damp hair wrapped in a towel.

"Open the door, dearie. We're getting late. The Ball will be starting soon."

"Mrs. Merryweather, I don't want to, I mean I can't go to the Ball," Ella said opening the door. "What's this?"

"This my dear, is your costume," Mrs. Merryweather said pushing her aside to enter. "You've got to get dressed. Hurry up!"

"But... but... what's this?" Ella asked confused.

"Well, 'this' belonged to one of my goddaughters long ago. I've brought it for you. You've got to get dressed. We don't have much time," Mrs. Merryweather said taking the costume out from the layers of tissue it was wrapped in.

"Mrs. Merryweather!" gasped Ella. "I... I... can't wear this."

"Of course you can, and you are going to. Please hurry and get into it. We're getting late. I've got to do your hair too. Where's your hair dryer and the curler?" Mrs. Merryweather queried.

~

Ella walked up the marble stairs of the grand entrance of the castle. She could hardly recognize the place. It looked amazing. Breathtaking floral arrangements, candles and gauzy drapes had completely transformed the entire place. Dim pink, blue and white lights gave it the appearance of fairyland. She walked down the carpeted corridors and reached the ballroom. The guards in livery gave her haughty but appreciative looks before they pushed open the massive doors engraved with delicate patterns and the family insignia.

Ella drew a deep breath as the sound of music, laughter and the happy chatter met her ears. And then suddenly... the entire room went silent.

Everyone in the room was staring at her!

She slowly stepped into the room and smiled uncertainly. Andrew who had been talking to the guests smiled and stepped forward to welcome her. Ella glanced at him before dropping her eyes and curtseying, he looked handsome dressed like a prince who had just stepped out from a fairytale. People dressed as fairies, witches, wizards, skeletons and others resumed their discussions once again.

"Good evening, Lord Whitman," Ella whispered nervously.

"Good evening, Miss Wilson. Please allow me to compliment you on your appearance. You look beautiful!"

"Thank you," Ella murmured and blushed.

At just that moment the band struck a chord. The lights grew dim in the room. People started walking to the dance floor with their partners.

"May I have this dance with you, Miss Wilson?" asked Andrew stretching out his hand for hers.

"Yes," whispered Ella with a shy smile.

"May I?" Andrew enquired placing his arm around her waist just as the singer began singing Calum Scott's You are the Reason.

Ella nodded, hardly daring to speak. Andrew drew her gently onto the dance floor. He held her close as they swayed together. She smelt of roses and he inhaled the soft fragrance appreciatively. He smiled as he felt her quiver in his arms. His Ella was melting...

"Everyone's staring at me," she finally murmured.

"Yes, because you're looking exquisite," he whispered back.

Ella concentrated on keeping up with his steps unaware of what a delightful picture she presented to all who had gathered there, in the salmon pink and peach tulle gown. It shimmered delicately when she moved as if the rays of the dying sun had been gently woven into the fabric. Her dark brown waist length hair was arranged in soft curls that fell about her shoulders in dark waves. The rosebuds and baby's breath in her hair added to her innocent beauty. Tiny pearls fell from her ears while her neck and wrists were bare. The flowing bell sleeves gave her an ethereal quality.

"Do I? She questioned, looking at his face in surprise.

"Yes. Don't you believe me?"

Ella made a small unintelligible sound as she circled the floor in his arms, now to Ed Sheeran's Perfect.

"Don't they look perfect together?" Mrs. Merryweather asked Hannah who stood beside her. Both of them were watching their favourite couple dance.

"Yes, absolutely!" Hannah said wiping tears from her eyes.

~

Ella lost track of time and space. She felt she was floating on a cloud, dreaming a joyous dream. The entire evening had passed in a happy haze. She had spent almost every moment either in Andrew's company or in his arms dancing. He hadn't left her side for more than a couple of moments. He tended to her most tenderly, getting her delicious bites and a glass of wine or water, whatever she desired.

The band played the last song of the night, Engelbert Humperdinck's The Last Waltz. Andrew drew her closer as they danced again and buried his face in her hair. He didn't want the evening to end. He guided her to the French windows and out onto the balcony. A full moon shone resplendently in the sky.

"Ella..." he whispered stepping away from her and tugging at her hand. "Come with me."

"Where? What about all of them?" Ella queried, looking back at the room full of people.

"Do you trust me?"

"Yes..." she breathed.

"Come..." he gently guided her through the private Rose Garden fragrant with the last roses and early chrysanthemums. The fountains tinkled softly in the silvery darkness.

They walked through the carefully laid out garden, lovingly tended by the devoted staff. Her sequined slippers with low heels shimmered in the moonlight as she lifted her full skirts with the other hand.

"Are we going to the lake?" Ella asked softly.

"Yes, I want to show you something," Andrew said holding her hand firmly in his.

Ella stopped short and gasped when the lake came into view. The archaic wooden bridge had been decorated just like the castle. Delicate floral arches had been set up at both the ends. The Moon scattered her most precious diamonds on the lake and they sparkled in the dark. A pair of swans glided on the perfectly still surface of the water just then and engaged in a love dance. Andrew drew her onto the bridge. He turned to look at her beautiful face shining with happiness.

"What do you think?" he asked softly.

"It's beautiful," she whispered.

"But not more than you, Ella. You surpass everything," Andrew took a step closer and looked into her eyes.

Ella's breath caught in her throat as he bent his head and pressed a soft kiss on her lips.

"I've wanted to do this all evening," he said softly against her lips.

Her lips trembled beneath his and she shivered.

He raised his head to look at her face. "Are you cold?

She shook her head looking into his eyes.

"Good," he whispered before claiming her lips again.

He gently placed his hands around her narrow waist and drew her into his warmth. Her arms rose to gently wind themselves around his neck as she leaned against him. Andrew deepened the kiss when she sighed and gave herself to him in that moment.

Time stood still and so did the Moon in the sky. In fact, the Moon blushed and tried to cover her face with a few wisps of clouds.

The Clock in the castle's tower however seemed unaware of how desperately Time wanted these precious moments to continue endlessly. It began striking midnight loudly in the stillness of the night.

Ella was startled and drew back hastily. She glanced at him with a dazed expression. And, before Andrew could move or stop her she picked up her full skirts and fled nimbly into the darkness like a gazelle.

"Good morning, Andrew. How are you?"

"Good morning, Mrs. Merryweather. I'm good. How's Ella?"

"Ella...? I met her yesterday. She came to return the gown. She looked fine. Is something wrong?" Mrs. Merryweather asked.

"No... No. I was just asking. Actually I haven't spoken to her since the night of the Ball. So..." Andrew said into the phone.

"Did something happen?"

"Well... yes... and no."

"What's that supposed to mean?"

"I mean there's nothing to be alarmed about. That's what I'm hoping. But I don't know."

"Andrew... you're not making much sense. Will you tell me what happened?"

"On the night of the Ball... I took her for a quiet walk to the lake and perhaps I misjudged her interest in me... I don't know. She was looking so beautiful. I couldn't resist the temptation and..." Andrew hesitated.

"You kissed her?" Mrs. Merryweather asked softly.

"Well, yes. I don't know. Did I mess up? Have I ruined my chances with her?" Andrew asked anxiously.

"You kissed her? Mrs. Merryweather asked happily. "In the middle of the lake, under the night sky? How romantic!"

"Mrs. Merryweather... that's what... What? What did you just say?" Andrew asked surprised. "You think it's romantic? You don't think I shouldn't have?"

"Of course you should have! It's romantic. Which girl wouldn't feel some butterflies?"

"But she just turned and ran away."

"Did she yell at you? Did she slap you?"

"No... No... I don't remember her yelling at me or even looking at me angrily. She looked... She looked... surprised..." Andrew said trying to remember clearly.

"My boy! You've got to talk to her, don't bear down on her but let her feel your presence around. Keep close to her but not that close. Don't suffocate her; give her space to make her decision. Let her process her feelings," Mrs. Merryweather advised.

"You mean I should meet her and talk to her?"

"Yes, but keep it impersonal."

"Alright. I'll go to the cafe now," Andrew said looking at his wrist watch.

"Great! I wish you all the best," Mrs. Merryweather said. "God! I'm so, so happy, Andrew!"

"Thank you, Mrs. Merryweather," Andrew laughed. "Goodbye!"

Mrs. Lucia Merryweather put down the cell phone and looked at her friend.

"So, Andrew kissed Ella in the castle grounds? Congratulations, Lucia!" Gabriella said from where she sat at the table. She raised her coffee mug in salutation.

"Isn't it wonderful? My dear, dear Ella. My darling goddaughter... Ella," Mrs. Merryweather said tears streaming down her face. "I'm so happy for her, for them."

~

"Hi..."

"Hello..." Ella smiled at Andrew when he walked into the cafe. Andrew smiled back breathing a sigh of relief.

"How are you?" he asked taking off his shades. He looked at the woman he loved with his whole heart. He tried not to show how much, just now. He had to be careful or else he might scare her away.

"I'm good. How are you?"

"I'm good too. Still quite a crowd," Andrew observed and nodded in approval.

"Yes, we're busy. I guess they'll be around for another day or two before they start moving back," Ella said wiping her hands on her jeans. "Would you like to have a cup of coffee?"

"No... Could we speak for a couple of moments?" Andrew asked.

"Yes, sure. Hannah..." Ella called.

When Hannah looked her way she signalled to her asking her to take over at the counter. Hannah smiled broadly and waved as Andrew escorted Ella out of the cafe.

"Shall we walk, just a short distance?" Andrew asked helping her with her jacket. He tried not to think of kissing her lips. She looked so cute wearing that pink pullover.

"Ok..." Ella said, forgetting to breathe when his fingers brushed her chin.

"Ella, I was wondering if we could plan a Christmas celebration here for those who'd like a vacation during the festival season. What do you think?"

"It would be a great idea. We do have a white Christmas every year. It would be lovely," Ella said considering his question.

"It's my first year as Lord Whitman, I want everything to be perfect here. I was thinking I'll invite my family to join me for Christmas," Andrew said as they walked along slowly.

The streets were still crowded. Couples and even families could be seen walking around.

"Your family? How lovely! You plan to celebrate Christmas here?"

"Yes. This is where I want to be for Christmas this year. I'm sure my mother and my two younger brothers and sister would love to be here too," Andrew smiled as he thought of them.

"That sounds like a great idea!" Ella said thinking of her mother and father wistfully.

"What happened? You sound sad," Andrew observed, stopping. He turned to look at her.

"Nothing... I was just thinking of mother and father," Ella smiled.

"I can understand..." Andrew said hugging her.

"I'm being silly! I have Hannah and Jim and Joe and now there's Mrs. Merryweather too," Ella laughed into his shoulder.

"No, you aren't being silly at all. Ella, I want to be here for the Christmas season and celebrate the festival with you and the others."

"Hmm..." Ella murmured into his jacket. This felt so good. She inhaled his citrus after shave and sighed.

"Alright! So that means I have to work hard so that I can give myself a holiday," Andrew said drawing back with regret. "I'll be going back tomorrow. I have a number of meetings lined up with important international clients. But I'll stay in touch. I'll call you. Will you speak to me Ella?"

Ella looked at him and nodded. "Yes."

"Well, then I'll see you sometime soon. Till then take good care of yourself. Right?" Andrew said cheerfully.

"Right. I'll do that. You take care too," Ella said smiling.

"I will. And, I must get my camera the next time I come. I missed the opportunity to take some lovely fall pictures," Andrew said tucking a wayward curl behind her left ear tenderly.

"Winter is even more beautiful. It's actually a winter wonderland. You'll get some really good pics," Ella said with a smile.

"I'm sure. Come. Let me walk you back to the cafe. Hannah will need you," Andrew said linking his fingers with hers and gently tugging.

"Mrs. Merryweather? All good? She doesn't know that I'm here. Right?" Andrew said peeping out of the window of the living room. "And, she did say she'll come?"

Mrs. Merryweather laughed at him. "This is the hundredth time you've asked me the same question, Andrew dear. Yes, she'll be coming. It's not yet seven. Don't worry she'll be here."

"Andrew, why are you so nervous? She left from the cafe at five. I made sure that we close down by four," Hannah said standing up from the sofa. "I'll just go and check the roast turkey."

"Alright... But suppose she doesn't come?"

"Andrew, how do you manage your business and deal with all those sharks in your world?" Mrs. Merryweather said standing with a hand on her hip.

"That's different, Mrs. Merryweather. This is Ella we're talking about," Andrew said pacing the room.

"Yes, I know. And, I also know that you two have been having long conversations over the phone," Mrs. Merryweather said with a smile.

"Yes, we've been in touch."

"And... You think she has feelings for you as you have for her," Mrs. Merryweather said. "Yes?"

"Yes... I think so."

"Very good. So, here we are then to watch her expressions and gauge her reaction to seeing you here on Thanksgiving. A surprise for her, no doubt!" Mrs. Merryweather said smiling.

"What's the plan, Andrew?" Hannah queried walking in.

"If all's well tonight during the Thanksgiving meal, I'll invite her over to the castle tomorrow for lunch and pop 'the' question," Andrew said standing in the middle of the room.

"Oh... that would be wonderful!" Hannah and Mrs. Merryweather chorused.

"And, how soon would you plan to... I mean..." Mrs. Merryweather asked wiping a tear.

"Christmas wouldn't be too soon? Would it?" Andrew asked looking at these two ladies who had been his pillars of support throughout.

"Not at all!" Hannah said happily.

"No... No... Not at all," Mrs. Merryweather said merrily.

"I thought so too... I wish I could make her mine sooner," Andrew said sitting down. "I don't know how I would have got this far without both of you."

"Hush now! No need for all this..." Hannah said. "There goes the doorbell. Andrew, you better open the door."

~

"Good afternoon, Miss Ella. How nice to meet you again," Mathew said with a broad smile. "Did you enjoy your walk in the gardens?"

"Good afternoon, Mathew. Yes, and I'm utterly famished. I feel I can eat an elephant," Ella laughed.

"Clara hasn't prepared an elephant but we have other delectable delights for you and Lord Whitman," Mathew said with a flourish.

"Bring them on, Mathew. We're starving," Andrew said eagerly.

"In a bit, Sir. First, please do justice to this carrot ginger soup. It's excellent for the cold weather," Mathew said placing the soup before them. Bon appétit!"

"Hmm... this is delicious," Ella said tasting some. "Please tell Clara, I love the soup."

"Surely, Miss Ella. Clara will be happy. I'll fetch the next course," Mathew said and left with a bow.

Dish after dish was brought in and served with great love. Mathew coaxed her to try the creamed Brussels sprouts and the stuffed mushrooms in a fatherly fashion. He smiled when he saw her enjoying her meal.

"That's all, I don't think I can eat another morsel, Mathew. I've no place for dessert now," Ella finally said ruefully.

"What's for dessert, Mathew?" asked Andrew. "I'm just asking, even though I feel like Ella. I'm stuffed like a Christmas turkey."

"Clara has made apple pie sorbet for dessert, my Lord!" Mathew said with a knowing smile.

"Ohh... I simply love that," Andrew groaned. "Do you think we could have it after dinner?"

"No problem, Sir. I'll tell Clara. But... Miss Ella? Will she?" Mathew looked at Andrew.

"Ella, you just can't afford to miss out on this dessert. I know, I asked you to have lunch with me, but could I be bold enough to ask you to do me the honour and also accompany me for dinner tonight," Andrew asked earnestly.

"Well... if it's to have Clara's food and heavenly dessert... I can't say 'no'. I'll stay for dinner," Ella said solemnly even though her eyes danced.

"That would be wonderful! Mathew, please tell Clara I'm indebted to her for life," Andrew said laughing.

"Yes, sir. Clara will be pleased, Miss Ella," Mathew said.

"Mathew, could you get us some coffee in my study? I challenged Ella to a game of scrabble and she accepted. After this delicious meal, I feel drowsy and I'll need to stay awake. Some good, strong coffee would be just the thing to keep me alert," Andrew said standing up and helping Ella to her feet.

"In a trice, Sir."

"Come, Ella. You really think you can defeat me?" Andrew asked mischievously.

"Try me, Lord Whitman," Ella said with a lift of her chin.

"Good... I like a spirited opponent. Let's go then."

~

"You're doing well, Lord Whitman. Nice word," Ella said frowning.

"Yes? What are you going to make?" Andrew said trying to have a look at the letters she had.

"I think... H-E-A-R-T. Yes, that's it," Ella said placing the letters on the board.

"Beautiful word. And, I therefore, I can now make... L-O-V-E. Now, that's precious, isn't it?"Andrew said.

"Yes, love is a precious emotion," Ella peeked at his face from under her lashes.

"Your turn, Ella."

"T-R-U-S-T"

"Hmm... that's important in any relationship, it's far more essential that love. Initially you didn't trust me at all, Ella. I hope you do a little bit now?" Andrew queried looking at her.

"Lord Whitman... What a time to ask something like this?" Ella said.

"I know. Let's continue. But you do trust me a little bit?" Andrew asked again.

"Lord Whitman, that would be an understatement. I trust you quite a lot," Ella said seriously.

"And, still you insist on calling me 'Lord Whitman'? Why not call me Andrew? It doesn't sound that bad," Andrew teased her.

"Aren't we playing anymore?" Ella enquired with a raised eyebrow. "In that case I guess I've won. My scores read more than yours."

"No... Who said we aren't playing? It's my turn, isn't it? Alright... P-R-O-P-O-S-E." Andrew said looking at Ella with a smile.

"Great. Then... R-O-S-E. I think that makes a proposal more romantic," Ella said smiling at him.

"Really?"

"Hmm... It makes everything more beautiful," Ella said shrugging her shoulders.

"Yes... Yes. A rose," Andrew nodded. "I just thought of something. I have an important call to make. I'll just come."

"Now? What happened suddenly?"

"I'll just come. Excuse me for a few minutes," Andrew said.

"Lord Whitman..."

"I'm coming..."

~

"Hi!"

"Hello..." Ella responded. "Where did you go?"

"I just remembered something. I'm sorry. I'm glad you found something to keep you busy in the library," Andrew said. "Shall we resume the game?"

"You still want to play?" Ella laughed.

"Just a little while more. Come... Come..." Andrew escorted her to the study.

"Lord Whitman..." Ella laughed again. "You seem to be bent on completing this game of scrabble, I wonder why."

"Yes, come on in. Let's do it," Andrew said pushing open the door of the study.

"Alright. So who's turn it was to make a word?"

"Yours."

"No, not mine. I had made the word R-O-S-E. Remember?"

"Have a look at the board," Andrew urged her.

Ella smiled and looked at the board and then gasped.

"Will you marry me?" Andrew slowly read what was written on the scrabble board.

Ella's eyes flew to his face. "I... I...."

Andrew reached in his pocket and took out a single rose blossom. He went down on his knee and repeated, "Ella Wilson, will you marry me?"

"A rose? Is that the reason you disappeared?" Ella asked surprised.

"Well, how could I not? Ahem... You've still not answered and my knee's sort of hurting," Andrew said wincing comically.

Ella laughed and carefully placed the required letters on the board. "Y-E-S... Yes. I'll marry you."

"Wow! I love you, Ella. I can't wait to begin living my life with you," Andrew said rising and kissing her. "I only hope with time you'll begin loving me a little bit too."

"I already love you, Lord... I mean Andrew."

"Finally, Andrew!" Andrew rolled his eyes and laughed. "You really love me?"

Ella nodded with tears of joy shining in her eyes.

"Oh darling!" He kissed her again and then said. "I also have a ring for you. It's a family heirloom. I brought it from my mother before I came here. I hope you'll like it."

"You had planned all this?" Ella asked incredulously.

"Guilty! Here... Have a look at it," Andrew opened the tiny jewel box. "What do you think?"

"It's exquisite," Ella exclaimed softly. "I love it."

"May I?" he asked before placing it on her finger. "It's exquisite, just like you."

Ella admired the blood red ruby heart in the centre with a circle of diamonds around it.

She rose on her tiptoes to kiss him. "Thank you." She whispered against his lips.

"For what?"

"This lovely surprise, this ring, the rose..." Ella began to count.

"Wait a minute... Add 'inviting Mrs. Merryweather and Hannah to join in our happiness at dinner tonight' to your list," Andrew said hugging her.

"You invited them? To dinner? With us? But when?" Ella drew back in surprise to stare at his face.

"Well, I made a phone call or two before I actually asked you..." Andrew said sheepishly. "And, they had been in on this..."

"Do you mean to say that they had been planning and plotting with you...?" Ella looked at him more incredulously than before.

"I'm grateful that they did. I can't imagine my life without you," Andrew said smiling at her.

"Yes, neither can I," Ella smiled back.

"How soon will you be willing to be my wife?" Andrew asked bending his head to claim her lips.

"How soon are you willing to take me as your wife?"

"I can't wait but I think Christmas would be a great time. Our friends and family would be with us," Andrew whispered.

"Andrew... you had this all planned. Didn't you? Long back..." Ella shook her head at him.

"Are you complaining, my lady?"

"Not at all, my lord."

"Good..." Andrew said before capturing her lips in a soul searching kiss.

Epilogue

The entire town gathered in the small church of the beautiful town on Boxing Day. It had turned out to be a white Christmas after all. Everyone was dressed in their best. The town's favourite girl had found her Prince Charming.

The quaint church was decorated with evergreens, white chrysanthemums and imported dark red roses. Arches were set up by the decorators and draped with maroon and white lace and ribbons. The entire place smelt of incense, pine leaves and the flowers. Pretty white candles lit up the beautiful altar.

Soon the church bells began to peal merrily. The choir rendered 'I'll never find another you' in their angelic voices as Ella walked down the aisle with the Mayor. She smiled at Andrew who stood at the altar looking at her lovingly.

"She looks stunning, doesn't she, Mrs. Merryweather?" Hannah observed. "That gown and veil so become her."

"Yes, she looks ethereal," said Mrs. Merryweather. "Its love that makes her glow, Hannah."

"Yes. You're right," Hannah whispered.

Ella had eyes for no one else except the man she loved, just like him. She looked radiant in white. The full skirt of her gown made of the finest tulle looked as if it had been woven from the moon's beams. Hundreds of pearls and sparkling stones patterned the closely fitted bodice. The leg of mutton sleeves gave her the appearance of a sixteenth century princess. Her veil, a wisp of the softest clouds held in place by the Whitman family tiara was carried by two bridesmaids. One of whom was Andrew's sister and the other a cousin. Both the girls were dressed in pretty maroon gowns.

When she reached the altar, Andrew fitted out in an immaculate greyish-blue suit and crisp white shirt stepped forward to take her hand. The family's gold cufflinks peeped out at his wrists and screamed class. She handed her bouquet made of the winter evergreens, roses and chrysanthemums to Andrew's sister with a smile.

"Dearly beloved, we have gathered here this morning to witness this man and woman be united in holy matrimony..." the Pastor began.

Ella felt the comforting warmth of Andrew's hand. She remembered that less than twenty-four hours ago she had felt terrified to think of her role as the new Lady Whitman. She realized she would be expected to play hostess to his business partners and friends and family. Her heart melted when she recollected how gently Andrew had put her mind to rest. She turned to smile at him. The Pastor had just announced that the couple would now take their marital vows.

Andrew picked up the smaller of the two simple gold bands Ella had specially chosen for both of them from the tiny tray an altar boy was holding. He took a deep breath, smiled at her and said in a solemn voice, "I, Andrew Anderson Whitman, take you, Ella Wilson to be my lawfully wedded wife, to have and to hold, from this day forward, for better, for worse, for richer, for poorer, in sickness and in health. Until death do us part!"

He placed the ring on her finger. Then it was Ella's turn.

She made her vows with deep devotion in a voice she barely recognized and placed a similar gold band on his finger too.

The Pastor blessed the couple and said, "I pronounce you man and wife. You may kiss the bride."

Andrew gently raised her veil to kiss her tenderly on her lips as the entire congregation clapped enthusiastically. Andrew's family sitting in the family pew beamed at him and Ella while his sister hugged her and whispered in her ear, "Welcome to the family, Ella."

The rest of the service passed as if in a dream and soon they were walking out as husband and wife from the Church. Everyone showered them with flower petals and confetti. A renowned photographer with his team was capturing pictures and videos to immortalize these moments for a lifetime.

~

The banquet hall in the castle gleamed with the bright lights from the sparkling chandeliers. The entire room was decorated in similar colours as the church. A huge Christmas tree stood decked with the brightest ornaments in a prominent corner. The entire town was there to wish the newlyweds a happy married life. They chatted happily, enjoying the wedding brunch.

"Congratulations, my dear girl," Andrew's mother hugged Ella and kissed her. "Welcome to the family.

"Thank you," Ella beamed. "Thank you for accepting me like a daughter."

"How could it be anything else, Ella? You're such a sweetheart."

"That she is," Mrs. Merryweather and Hannah said hugging her too.

Andrew just then said in a loud voice, "Your attention everyone, I would like to raise a toast to my beautiful wife whom I love so much. To my mother who has always stood by me through thick and thin. And, to two wonderful ladies who have been inseparable parts of this marriage ploy – Hannah, for silently supporting me and Mrs. Merryweather for being my fairy godmother more than Ella's! Cheers!"

"Now, I wonder how did he know that I'm her fairy godmother?" mumbled Mrs. Merryweather.

"What did you say, Mrs. Merryweather?" shouted Hannah above the thunderous applause and good wishes.

"Nothing... Nothing..." Mrs. Merryweather said clapping with the others.

~

Ella stood on the balcony and looked at the snow covered garden sparkling in the weak winter sunshine.

"It's cold to stand out here, darling. Come in," Andrew came and stood behind her. He placed his hands on her shoulders.

"Yes, in a minute. I was just thinking that not so long ago I was showing you this balcony and telling you about the castle. And, then I was visiting you as a guest and today..."

"Today... you're Lady Whitman," Andrew turned her around and gently traced her face with a finger. "It was destined, Ella. You're my Anam Cara. You remember I told you what it meant that day we played scrabble for the first time?"

"Soul friend..." whispered Ella as she closed her eyes at the pleasure of his touch.

"Yes, you're my soul friend, my love, my wife... my Ella." Andrew said drawing her closer in his arms and kissing her.

~

"Welcome back, Lucia. Congratulations on your goddaughter's marriage to her prince charming," Gabriella said happily. "How does it feel?"

"Thank you, Gabriella. It feels lovely of course to have another goddaughter happily married. I'm so glad Ella got her fairytale ending."

"Now you can contentedly say, '... and they lived happily ever after'. Right, Lucia?"

"Yes, oh yes!" Lucia said looking down from amongst the sparse clouds to see the couple kissing on the balcony.

Other Books by the Author

The Ferns and Blooms Trilogy

1. Magic at Ferns and Blooms
2. More Magic at Ferns and Blooms
3. Goodbye Ferns and Blooms

Love under the Gulmohar Series

1. Gulmohar Love
2. Gulmohar Valentine

Other Romance Novels

1. Mistletoe Magic

www.ingramcontent.com/pod-product-compliance
Lightning Source LLC
LaVergne TN
LVHW041217150826
845673LV00001B/438